Tales from the Upper Room

Tales from the Upper Room

Poems and Short Stories by the Canvey Writers, St Nicholas Group, who meet in the upstairs room...

Edited by Janice Gilbert, Debz Hobbs-Wyatt and Gini Scanlan

Proceeds from the sale of this book will be donated to Havens Hospices

Bridge House

British Library Cataloguing in Publication Data

A Record of this Publication is available from the British Library

ISBN 978-1-907335-19-8

This edition published 2017 by Bridge House Publishing Manchester, England

Canvey Writers
St Nicholas Group

"We will nurture and support local writers of all levels, and who write for all reasons, to achieve their own success; be that publication, winning competitions or simply the love of writing."

Contents

Foreword by Debz Hobbs-Wyatt

There are good writing groups and there are bad writing groups. I fortunately belonged to, and then went on to run, a good one, actually a great one, in Bangor, North Wales for a number of years. Given the often isolated nature of being a writer, I saw the impact that coming together as a group and supporting one another could have. At the time Bangor Cellar Writing Group was founded no one had had any publishing success. By the time I left to move back to Canvey Island, it boasted publishing successes and competition wins. That group, now more than ten years old, continues to achieve through its ethos of support and encouragement.

I left Wales three years ago to return to Canvey, where I was born and raised. One of the first things I wanted to do was join a writing group. However, the island only boasted one group, who meet at Canvey library during the day, and day times don't work so well for me as I am a full-time writer and editor. So, I decided to start an evening one. Canvey Writers, St Nicholas Group, was born in January 2015 and has gone from strength to strength. We do share members with the other group and enjoy a good relationship with them – and I was thrilled to see just how much local creative writing talent there is.

Canvey Writers St Nicholas Group has over twenty members and most of those who joined us at that first meeting are still with us and beginning to have publishing successes! I was quite certain when we started I wanted to create a supportive environment to nurture both beginners and advanced writers. "Leave egos at the door," I said, "as this is about helping one another – no matter how much or how little writing you have done before." I think that ethos I borrowed from Bangor has worked well in establishing a strong group. We have welcomed guest authors, held workshops and internal competitions and now this is our biggest venture yet.

The group decided when it celebrated its second birthday, back in January 2017, that as well as a showcase evening for charity (with the other Canvey group) to show off our work, they wanted to publish an anthology. Because I work with Dr Gill James over at Bridge House Publishing, short story specialists, I put it to her and she agreed we would publish the collection – launched at our showcase evening.

As a group we also decided that the proceeds of the launch event, as well as any profits made from the sale of this collection, would go to a local charity. We all agreed on Havens Hospices that do incredible work at both the adult hospice, Fairhavens, and the children's hospice, Little Havens, in Essex. The latter I have visited and cannot tell you how humbling that was. So we are delighted that they will receive the profit from the sale of every copy.

What you will read is quite an eclectic mixture of poems, flash fiction (some in only one hundred words) and longer short stories. Some of these were written in response to prompts set within the group, in the upstairs room at St Nicholas Church, Long Road. Some were penned for pure fun. Some of the tales, and yes even poems tell tales, are dark, while others add a touch of humour. Some of the writers are new and this is their publishing debut; some are more experienced. When we decided to publish a collection, we also formed a critique group and helped one another improve their work. So please do remember most of the writers have not been published before and this collection, we hope, is only the beginning.

Most importantly it shows what a little group like ours

is capable of – and maybe you are sitting at home thinking how you have always wanted to write, well maybe this will inspire you to join us or a group near you. All that remains now is to say, please enjoy the work of the Canvey Writers...

Debz ☺

Author/Editor/Publisher/Founder of Canvey Writers St Nicholas Group

Mavis, Cuddles and the End of the World

Alan Jacobson

World War III started at 7:27 pm on 11th May; it was a Thursday but, before I alarm you unnecessarily, dear reader, I should clarify that the cataclysmic events to which I refer, occurred, not in the real here and now, but in the virtual world that is *Other Life*.

"You haven't really lived until you've lived your Other Life," stated the announcer for the online ad that Mavis had clicked on.

"Be the person you always wanted to be," it continued.

Up to a few seconds earlier, Mavis had been looking at videos of cute cats but had been side-tracked by one of those 'clickbait' links always present on web pages these days.

The advertisement from The Genesis Corporation was for a "Brand new virtual experience."

The announcer went on to explain that, for a reasonable monthly charge Mavis could be one of the thousands of people worldwide who had already signed up to this twenty-first century phenomenon that was taking the world by storm – but to hurry as this was a once in a lifetime offer.

Intrigued, Mavis drank a few more mouthfuls from her second glass of red Lambrusco and watched on.

As soon as the video had finished, Mavis clicked on the link, signed up and purchased her new existence in *Other Life*.

Two days later all the paraphernalia: virtual headset, DVD, cables, controllers, password and documentation arrived by courier at the solicitors where she worked in the word processing department. With just a little bit of help from Steve in IT, Mavis had installed the software on her laptop and was ready to go.

Mavis Bracegirdle had lived alone since her mum died; alone that is if you didn't include her seven cats. The wrong side of forty, and dress size twelve a distant memory, thanks mainly to a diet of junk food and chocolate, she appeared a lonely figure. She'd never had a boyfriend – well not since Colin when she was seventeen, and even he hadn't been what you'd really call a boyfriend. They'd only gone out the once, to the pictures, where he'd tried to get his hand in her knickers in the middle of *Indiana Jones and the Last Crusade*. She'd stood up with a shriek, tipping most of a shared giant tub of buttered popcorn over a crestfallen Colin. Running out of the cinema, she'd never again set foot in one since that night.

Mavis finally got to see the whole film when it had been on the telly a few weeks back. Even after all these years, it had immediately brought back memories of that night: Harrison Ford, the smell of buttered popcorn and Colin's short-lived fumblings; she'd idly mused that these days she might quite like a hand in her knickers.

The cinema incident had put her off men for a while and then her mother got ill; a mean spirited, self-centred person at the best of times, she had turned into a demanding, selfish harridan and it was a relief for Mavis to escape the house to go to work each day. The demands of her mother in the evenings precluded any sort of social life but, ill or not, the old witch had hung on for another twenty-odd years, and it wasn't until she'd just turned forty-one that Mavis was finally free of her.

By the time she buried her mother, she'd just simply got used to not having a social life and, lacking in self-confidence, wasn't even sure she'd know how to start one.

14

The other girls in WP had always tried to coax her out for a drink on a Friday night and involve her in their out of work activities but Mavis had always cried off, citing her sick mother as the reason. Since Mum died, she'd started using the cats as her excuse for rushing home. She was affable and friendly enough with the other girls: joining the lottery syndicate, bringing cakes in on her birthday and sponsoring their charity walks – all the usual stuff of office life – but at going home time she had done just that and gone home.

The day the software was installed, Mavis travelled home on the tube, aware of a frisson of excitement as she felt the weight of the laptop in her bag. She arrived home burdened down with a takeaway pizza she'd stopped off for, a bottle of red Lambrusco and a family size bar of Cadbury's Dairy Milk. Struggling through the front door, she pushed it shut with her backside, narrowly avoiding tripping over two of the cats as they attempted to weave between her legs. Dumping her purchases on the kitchen counter, she made a fuss of the cats that were present, filling the bowls with dry food and, while a few more cats drifted in through the cat flap in the kitchen door, checked and refilled a couple of water bowls.

Cats fed and watered, she grabbed a wineglass and carried her evening meal into the living room. Shucking off her coat, she let it fall to the floor, where it was immediately claimed by one of the cats. She plopped onto the sofa and set about pouring the wine and pulling off a wedge of pepperoni pizza. Mouth full of pizza, she pulled her laptop out of her bag, opened it and switched it on.

Since placing her order she had avidly read the forums of other users and discovered all sorts of useful stuff. For instance, in the alternate reality world, all the usual laws of physics still applied, so, just as in the real world, no one could fly or have super powers and, when a user was not signed in, their avatar waited to be animated like some lifeless virtual puppet.

Before putting on the VR headset she went to the online store to pick out and personalise an avatar, which she named Emma Stone. Emma was a dress size ten and looked remarkably like Mavis herself had at the time of the cinema, knickers, popcorn episode. Avatar designed, Mavis followed the instructions to upload Emma into the system and, switching on the wireless headset, with some trepidation, put it on.

And from the very first time she hesitantly walked into the universe that was *Other Life,* she felt she had come home.

Over the next few years Mavis created in Emma Stone the complete antithesis of herself: a confident, attractive and gregarious twenty-something, world-class, (well, *Other Life* world-class), gymnast who regularly represented her nation in the sport. This gave Mavis the opportunity to live vicariously through Emma and experience a life she would not otherwise have enjoyed.

A keen and enthusiastic citizen of Freedonia (the fictitious country Emma inhabited), Mavis had crafted a much loved, admired and respected member of the virtual community; indeed she had even pursued and now enjoyed an intimate relationship – as intimate as one could be in a virtual world – with Guy Manley. Guy had, in a landslide victory, just been elected President of Freedonia. In reality, Guy was Kenny Pratt, a flatulent, greasy, twenty-stone security guard from Rhyl with a dodgy comb-over.

Following Guy's election victory, a huge inaugural ball had been planned and was being held at the virtual

Government House. Naturally, as Emma was Guy's significant other she'd been invited to sit alongside him at the main table while he gave his acceptance speech. She'd arrived early and was shown into the Round Office – Freedonia's equivalent of the Oval Office. Mavis didn't know it at the time but Guy was being briefed by his defence chief on the intricacies of their nation's nuclear deterrent launch system. As this was a social function, the defence chief wasn't in uniform, instead she was wearing a strapless black ball gown which barely restrained her enormous breasts. Freedonia was an equal opportunities nation after all so why shouldn't the defence chief be a stunningly beautiful woman called Norma Stitz? As a side note, Norma was in real life a pre-op transgender sex worker from Dudley called Barry – but I digress.

To Mavis's insecure eyes, the tableau that presented itself appeared to be a way too intimate tête-à-tête. Mavis's self-doubt took over and, immediately leaping to the wrong conclusion, she experienced what can only be described as a crisis of faith in herself and the *life* she had created.

Back in the real world, sitting on the sofa of her ground floor flat, Mavis was in shock. Reaching up to snatch the virtual headset off, she accidentally knocked over the generous, nearly full glass of Lambrusco that had been on the arm of the sofa, emptying its entire contents over a soundly sleeping Cuddles, one of the aforementioned cats. Now, if ever a creature had been misnamed it was he. Cuddles was neither good-natured nor cuddly, in fact he was one of the most miserable animals one could ever have the misfortune to encounter, only tolerating Mavis because she fed him.

So, given Cuddles' temperament, it would be something of an understatement to say he was not best pleased at being woken from a deep sleep, quite understandably taking exception to the entire contents of a glass being dumped on him. In a display of agility that belied his advancing years, he leapt up with a hiss and a howl and darted across the coffee table where Mavis had her laptop. Scrabbling over the keyboard, his feet managed to hit the precise key sequence required to propel Emma, at great speed, into the Round Office. Hurtling towards the two occupants, she hit them with such force that all three tumbled onto the floor where, in the resulting melee, one of Norma's voluminous breasts unfortunately escaped from her strapless gown and accidentally pressed the launch button.

As this was supposed to be just a demonstration of the system, the missiles had been targeted on Gigantia, the largest nation in the whole of the *Other Life* universe. Gigantia had, up to this moment, been an ally and strong trading partner of Freedonia – indeed its ambassador was attending tonight's inaugural ball.

Events took their course – Gigantia retaliated as did their allies, likewise Freedonia's allies and, over the space of a very few minutes, the peaceful world of *Other Life* was destroyed.

Footnote:
The Genesis Corporation are currently creating *Other Life II.*

Mavis Bracegirdle's application for membership has been declined.

100 Worder: My Other Self

Peter Sandling

I have fought him for so long, this other person in my head. He was my equal but now begins to dominate. I cower from him and become weaker each day to his evil demands. I cannot resist. As my will slowly sinks into the abyss, his surges. He forces us into the street, but I rally. My mind soars bright and clear. He cackles inside me, slices of life peeling back. He forces me into the alley, his refuge, not mine. Weakness slows my mind and feet. This is my life to throw away. Cardboard castle, my home now.

Ethical Romance

Amber Graelin

For too long now
feelings of deep suppression
and mild depression have consumed me;
devoured my soul and wild spontaneous acts
upon which my life once was based.

For too long,
walls of every kind have surrounded me
and inadvertently crowded my mind
with ridiculousness that needn't be recalled,
but collapsed and destroyed completely.

Something now seems changed for the better.
Changed with the world, or my life
or us – definitely.
Every part of every part is now put into perspective.

Inadequacies I see
seem now to construct the true beauties and virtues
that before were previously hidden.
All my imperfections and flaws fly away now.

With those eyes in which I seek comfort and love,
I find all the best things plus more;
and bliss of the heart brings thoughts of a future;
a future I've never thought could be a possibility
until I realised the passion and pureness we share.

Resolutions of a pleasant nature this year
Pass my lips as a promise.
A promise to know better than be consumed and crowded.
A promise of happiness and serenity.
I give to you my promise of undying love in ethical romance.

Dedication: NCJW, this poem is dedicated to you; my best friend and love of my life. Thank you for everything, forever. HMTW.

Impetuous Jack – A Cautious Tale

Dave Traer

Jack was an impetuous soul;
Full of vigour, never dull.
What made him bad was not his pace,
Nor his zest, or need for space;
But the fact, he rarely slept;

And never looked before he leapt.

Jack was, by day, a testing child,
Making trouble, running wild.
By night, when he should have slept,
Jack, often from his bedroom crept.
His mother's words he would not hear,
His father's hand was never near.

Fate turned its hand against young Jack,
One fine day, behind his back.
With school ahead and woods behind,
The words, 'No contest', came to mind.
Jack turned his heels towards the trees,
And quickly moved his knobbly knees.

At last he came upon a field:
Pasture land, never tilled.
He saw the sign but could not read,
The words he was supposed to heed.
He leapt the fence, no fear at all
He should have read, 'Beware the Bull.'

Jack ran and ran, alive and free.
Weary, yet still full of glee.
Down with teachers, down with rules;
Down with silly, stupid schools;
Up with being bad and wild.
Silly, stupid, wayward child!

He saw the bull but much too late,
As it thundered through a gate.
It hit poor Jack with such a whack,
That up he flew with aching back,
Over the hedge and into a ditch;
More than just a minor hitch.

He laid there thinking, 'It can't be long,
Before some good farmer comes along.'
But hours passed without a sound,
Except for wind along the ground.
Help was doubtful after all,
Perhaps, he should have gone to school.

Tiredness soon upon him crept,
At last in many days he slept.
A pity that he had to slumber,
He missed the woodsman with his lumber.
Still not to worry, sleep was needed,
His mother's words, he should have heeded.

Jack was found in evening fog
By a shepherd with his dog
Now Jack cries, "It isn't fair
To have to sit in wheelie chair."
When he finds he cannot sleep
He can only look, he cannot leap.

Soundtrack to a Love Affair

Gini Scanlan

'Livin' La Vida Loca' by Ricky Martin, release date 23rd March 1999

Another week over; another child-free weekend; another girls' night out. We are two single women, both divorced, both still searching for 'Mr Right'. We're in Aldershot. My friend works as a civilian at the military base and assures me there will be men. *Lots* of men.

"Too short?"

"Never too short with legs like yours!"

"Too much cleavage? I feel a bit tarty in this dress."

"We're going out on the pull, not to bloody church."

We enter a wine bar and my friend starts a running commentary on the patrons. I sip my drink and peep discreetly over the rim of my glass, assessing the quality of the talent on display. I glance at the reflected faces in the mirror behind the bar. Your eyes fix on mine. I smile and look away.

"Who's that?"

"Where?"

"At the bar – tall, dark hair. Don't look!"

"He's staring right at you."

"Has been all night…"

"George Clooney?"

"Yep."

"That's Corporal Rutherford. Nicholas. Nick. He's a keeper."

"What do you mean?"

"Yorkshireman – dead sexy voice – really deep – proper manly – and single – well recently divorced – just back

from Kosovo – he'll be gagging for it."
"There'll be no shortage of takers, he's gorgeous!"

We move on to a salsa club. It is dark and smoky inside. The Latin music pumps through my body. I know how to move, I can dance. The alcohol has made me giddy and I shed my inhibitions, performing steps and sequences from choreography memorised long ago. I am surprised when an arm slips around me from behind and you pull me against your body. The music plays on and you keep me firmly 'in hold', matching my steps. You spin me and I find myself in the arms of Corporal Rutherford. Our eyes lock. I place my hand on your chest and feel hard muscle beneath your shirt. You hold me close and take the lead as our bodies move in unison. We dance together all night.

'Dov'è l'amore' by Cher, release date 6th July 1999

My children are with their father. You take me to a colleague's wedding. The first sight of you in dress uniform leaves me breathless. The old stone church is stunning, the sun streaming through the stained glass windows, the pews adorned with white roses. You hold my hand throughout the ceremony. I observe your reactions and contemplate what the future holds for us. You introduce me to your friends. And then we dance.

I wake early to find you lying on your side beside me, your finger tip gently outlining the tattoo on my bare shoulder.
"Good morning beautiful."
"Were you watching me sleeping?"
"You were snoring."

"I don't snore! Oh my God, was I really?"

"It's a cute snore... not loud."

"How to make a girl feel good about herself!"

"Come here..." you slide me across the bed, "... and I'll make you feel good..."

Your lips touch my neck and I am unable to resist.

'I Wanna Love you Forever' by Jessica Simpson, release date 22nd April 2000

You are back from your first tour of Afghanistan. My parents have the children for a few days. You won't take me to the barracks so I drive to Hampshire and meet you at a hotel. You tell me that you are tired but the sun is shining so we walk into the drab town centre anyway, fingers linked. We take in the matinee performance of *Girl, Interrupted*. You call me 'soppy' for crying but hold me tight and kiss my tears away.

Back in the room our tongues intertwine and we tear at each other's clothes with trembling fingers. We tumble onto the bed in a tangle of limbs. You roll on top of me and your dog tags hit my nose as you bend forward to kiss me. We giggle. You stop and stare at me.

"God, I've missed you." You kiss the tip of my nose. "You look different."

Because I am completely and utterly besotted with you. I absolutely love you.

"Keep your eyes open – I want to watch you."

You hold my gaze and your tags between your teeth until the moment comes when you need to let go.

Exhausted by the intensity of your passion, I drift off with my head on your chest, hypnotised by the metronomic beat of your heart.

It is dusk when I awake. The late evening sun streams

through a gap in the curtains, lighting the motes floating in the air. I run my fingers lightly through the coarse dark hair on your chest and look up at your face. You are still sleeping. I wish I hadn't asked why you wear two identical tags. I consider the possibility of you being killed in action, the possibility of never seeing you again. I am not your next of kin – I wouldn't be informed. Nobody would know to tell me you were dead. I feel pressure building up in my chest and suppress a sob.

'I'm Outta Love' by Anastacia, release date 30th September 2000

The room is dark; I am encircled in your arms; we are dancing; laughing. You are watching me again, gazing deeply into my eyes. You have the longest, darkest eyelashes I have ever seen and the most amazing green irises.

"I love you, Nick."

"I know."

"You're supposed to say 'I love you too'."

"But I don't, sweetheart. I'm not going to lie to you. If it was going to happen it would've happened by now and it hasn't."

I bite my lip and focus on the wall behind you. I will not cry.

"I'm not your *happily ever after*. You're beautiful and sexy and I really like you – honestly, I think the world of you – but we don't have a future together – I'm on active duty and you've got your own life in Essex with three kids."

You bend and rest your forehead against mine. I will not cry.

"I'm sorry."

"We could move…"

27

"I don't want to be a father to your kids."
I will not cry.

'Can't Get You Out of My Head' by Kylie Minogue, release date 17th September 2001

I don't really dance any more. I am seeing someone and he is not the dancing type. He is steady and kind; he loves my children and he adores me. He has proposed and I have accepted but truthfully, my heart isn't in it. Every news bulletin, every mention of the nine eleven terror attacks makes me think of you. I can't sleep. I don't know where you are. I know that you will be on high alert but I don't know if you have already been deployed. The thought of you being in mortal danger distresses me. I hunt through your letters, searching for a BFPO address to write to. I linger over photos; protect your image from my unchecked tears. I deliberate writing to the last location I have for your regiment in the hope that my letter will reach you.

Just to know that you are safe. Just to know that you are still alive.

'Cry' by Kym Marsh, release date 19th April 2003

I give birth to a daughter. I examine her tiny, perfect features and wonder what she would have looked like if she was yours. It dawns upon me that I will never dance again. I think about the man who loves me and resolve to be grateful for him and to make the best future I can for my family.

'Happy' by Pharrell Williams, release date 21st November 2013

A message comes through via social media. I see your name and catch my breath. I click on the icon and go to your homepage. I maximise the profile picture and examine the features on the visage posted there. The hair is greying but the green eyes still sparkle; it is unmistakably you. I feel sick. My chest feels tight. I try to regulate my breathing. Why now?

Your communication is tentative.

Do you remember me?

I've spent half of my adult life trying to forget you.

I've been thinking about you a lot.

I've never stopped thinking about you.

I'd love to hear from you, to know what you're doing and how you are. You look well in your DP... you've hardly changed at all!

It's amazing what a good hairdresser and a soft focus lens can do for a girl.

My hands are shaking. My palms are damp and my pulse is racing. I read your message again. I delight in the words. My husband works away. The marriage is celibate, our relationship stale. I share my life with a man that I am fond of but have never truly loved. I yearn for excitement, for this light-headed feeling of rapture that you have always evoked within me. There can be no harm in responding, surely?

Your reply pings straight back.

I am so happy to hear from you!

You are retired from the army and now live quite locally to me. You are teaching in an FE college. You married in 2002. I am hurt to read that you adopted your wife's illegitimate child immediately after your wedding. You didn't want to be a father to *my* children. I am crushed when I read that you have two children of your own with her.

Mel has had an affair and she's leaving me.

So you thought you'd contact me? Did you think I would be of comfort?

Isn't it your birthday soon – do you want to go out for a drink?

You remembered my birthday. Coffee would be safer. In a public place.

'All of Me' by John Legend, release date 8th March 2014

I am aware that despite the innocence of our current liaison, my husband would not approve. I am infatuated but I do not dare add you as a friend on Facebook or follow you on Twitter in case I arouse his suspicions. You write to me every day, always to my work email address; this way we cannot be discovered. You flirt outrageously when you are happy and seek my counsel when things are going badly. Your estranged wife uses your children as a weapon in the battle you are waging. We have not spoken, but I remember your voice so clearly that I read your words in dialect. We have not met, but only because I am not sure that I can trust myself around you, even if we just meet for coffee. In a public place. I cannot discern what you want from me, a friend, a companion or simply an uncomplicated lover. You have made it clear that you want me, but I want more from you than just sex. I can get that anywhere. I don't want uncomplicated; I want all of you.

'Hideaway' by Kezia, release date 11th April 2014

Today is your birthday. I have agreed to meet you in a salsa bar for a quick drink after work, just to say 'hello', because I can't bear to think of you spending the entire day alone. I find a table in the corner and watch the door. I am curious to know if there is any chemistry between us after all of these years, if the attraction is still there. My stomach lurches when you walk in. I observe the slim, upright, grey haired man at the bar as you buy a beer and look around. Your eyes skim over me but you continue to scour the room, searching for the object of your desire. The overweight, middle-aged woman sitting alone with a lime and soda clearly isn't it.

Are you coming?

I'm already here; hiding in plain sight.

'Love Runs Out' by One Republic, release date 14th April 2014

I am working away this week. I arrange for dinner and a bottle of wine to be bought up to my room. Two glasses in, I call you.

"Hello?"

"It's me. Can you talk?"

"Yeah, of course. Blooming heck! I wasn't expecting this."

"If it's not convenient…"

"No, it's not that, this is good. Great. It's just a surprise after Friday."

"Friday?"

"You stood me up. On my birthday."

"No, I was there… you just didn't recognise me. You looked around, drank your pint and left."

"I didn't see you… why didn't you come over?"

You didn't *see* me. I wasn't wearing an invisibility cloak.

"You looked straight past me. I think that said it all."

"I don't understand."

"It doesn't matter. How are you?"

"Much better for speaking to you. Mel's been giving me a hard time over the kids…"

"What went wrong between you?"

31

"I don't know. When I met her she was stunning. Tall, slim, beautiful; quite quiet, you know? Kept herself to herself. Then she had the kids and the weight piled on... she's let herself go completely..."

You need to choose a different audience if you want to criticise the mother of your children for being overweight.

"Then about a year ago she started drinking. A lot."

I glance at the nearly empty bottle in front of me. You need to choose a different audience if you want to criticise your ex-wife for drinking.

"She suddenly found her voice. We were arguing all the time, over money, the kids, the housework... she didn't do anything around the house at all."

"Was she working? Full-time?"

"Yeah, we both were."

You need to choose a different audience if you want to criticise the woman you married for working full-time and not doing enough housework.

"So the root cause of your marital problems is that she's put on weight, drinks and isn't house-proud enough? I take it you are teetotal now then?"

"No..."

"It's not that your expectations are unrealistic?"

"Do you think I'm being unreasonable?"

"Er, yes! Just a bit. I can't believe you're that shallow, Nick. The man I remember wasn't that superficial."

"Then I'm not the man you remember."

"Obviously not."

'Right Here' by Jess Glynne, release date 6th July 2014

Another week over, another Sunday morning. It is a beautiful day. I am trying to rekindle the romance in my marriage. My husband and I have talked a lot; we have both been divorced before and whilst we accept that we might not be quite right for each other, we are alright. He doesn't know about you and I plan to keep it that way. There is nothing to tell – there is no harm in window shopping providing you don't touch the goods and there was definitely no touching. We have agreed to make time for each other and re-engage because our marriage is worth saving. Not just for our daughter but for our own sakes as well. We start salsa classes on Friday.

War Came

Henry Lewi

Then out of the spring and summer days the War came.
It came in the shape of grim helmeted men dressed in
    grey.
It came in the shape of iron monsters that rode over
    people, houses and our soldiers.
It came in the shape of shrieking war planes, dropping
    bombs and killing all around us.
We ran, we fell,
Some got up, many did not,
Still they came.
They killed; they advanced
They didn't stop until they met our Greatest General
He held their advance,
He grounded their planes
He froze their iron monsters.
Thank God for General Winter
Our Saviour.

American High School

Peter Sandling

He called me fat and punched my arm
It really hurt but I won't cry
I'll get him back one day, you'll see
I'll just be very, very sly.

Him and Jimmy pick on me
It's not my fault I'm bright and sharp
I'll get them back one day, you'll see
I'll creep up in the dark.

The two girls bet my thingy was small
I know it is and that hit home
I'll get them back one day, you'll see
With breathing on the phone.

The teacher made me look a fool
Today in class and that's no fun
I'll get them back today you'll see
I'll use my daddy's gun.

100 Worder: Poor Tilly

Julie Kendall

I knew he'd done it! I knew he'd poisoned my Tilly just because she'd scratched his new leather jacket. He took out revenge on her and she was sick for a week and he didn't seem bothered!

Poor Tilly, she wouldn't come in from the garden even, which Paul was pleased about. I liked her sitting on my lap and missed that. I enjoyed that more than half-hearted hugs from Paul.

Now he is sick, so he knows how Tilly felt! It wasn't just the drink he had last night; it could have been the cat food sandwich he ate.

Job Search

Margaret Potter

"Good Morning, Mr Montegroo. How is the job search going?"

"Er... How are you?"

"Never mind about me. I've had feedback from your recent interview for a trapeze artist. Apparently, you're afraid of heights. Not to mention your one leg."

Mr Montegroo listened with a half-cocked ear. He could see the red slash of mouth moving, the raised eyebrows, the red nails pointing.

Ever since he had been released from the boring sober-sided bank and a thirty-year commute in a pinstripe, he had wanted to laugh. Even when he told Dorothy that evening, over one of her burnt shepherd's pies and she had gasped, "The neighbours! My husband redundant!"

Mr Montegroo had been nothing if not diligent in his job search. He had pointed out the vacancy for brain surgeon, citing the stint at the butcher's counter he had done all those years ago.

"I don't think you qualify," said red slash of mouth, accommodating a choccie biscuit for elevenses.

Mr Montegroo nodded. "Long John Silver lookalike." He pointed to his one good leg and hospital regulation crutches. "I'll need a parrot."

Red slash of mouth stopped in its tracks. The eyebrows rose.

Back home, Dorothy had palpations and cremated Wednesday's stew.

"My husband in panto! The neighbours!"

At the job centre it was cause for celebration. A parrot

37

had been found, stuffed of course. The buff file was stamped CLOSED and red slash of mouth said triumphantly, "One less statistic."

The Fosdyke Challenger

Robert Parker

Toby Reynolds led a lonely life.

His wife had left him fifteen years ago, not for another man, but merely for a normal life, a life with the companionship of her husband, a comfortable life with holidays, friends and a few laughs, the sort of life other people enjoyed.

Sadly, Toby hardly noticed she was gone. His life continued as it had for the past five years and would continue for the next fifteen.

Until today, the culmination of twenty years' work.

"Will you come and have a coffee, Toby? We've plenty of time, they won't be announcing the winner for another half hour at least, seems there's been a late entry."

"No, thanks, Charley, you know I don't like leaving the bike on its own, you can bring me one back though, milk, two sugars please."

Toby returned to the contemplation of his life's work, his 1922, 498cc overhead valve, single cylinder, Fosdyke Challenger, TT racer. The very machine on which its millionaire designer, Lord Willoughby-Fosdyke, had won the Isle of Man Tourist Trophy in the same year.

The machine had been lying at the back of an old barn, untouched and unloved for years. Untouched and unloved until Toby had found it when he and his wife had spent a holiday nearby, their last holiday together.

From then on he dedicated his life to its restoration. Joining the Vintage Motor Cycle Club, he spent day after day in the club library researching every photograph and report of the 1922 race. Not much remained, but what did, he had seen. Eventually, after nearly a year, he was ready to start work.

Every evening he would return home from the office; he would hardly speak to his wife as he pored over photographs and manuals. Then he would lock himself in his garage. Alone with the Fosdyke Challenger.

As the years went by, the machine rose from the grave. The work was slow, everything had to be perfect. The original paint was matched from a tiny scrap on the inside of the tool box. The wheels, the engine and frame were rebuilt with infinite care. Everything had to be perfect. Now, here it was, on public view for the first time in possibly ninety years.

Toby knew only twelve Fosdykes were ever made, three now remained, one in a museum in Chicago, one in pieces in Switzerland, which he had tried unsuccessfully to buy, and his. His was the only perfectly original and running Fosdyke Challenger in the world.

So it was with quiet confidence that Toby watched the President of the Vintage Motor Cycle Club step forward and tap the microphone.

"Can you all hear me? Marvellous."

"Good afternoon, everyone. I'm so pleased to announce that we have over ten thousand enthusiasts here today. We have seen all the prizes awarded but one, and it is my pleasure, no honour, as President of our wonderful club, to announce the winner of our most prestigious award. Yes, the Arthur Worsley Memorial Cup, for the most original restoration."

Normally a taciturn man, Toby went over in his mind the short, but carefully prepared, acceptance speech he would soon be called upon to make. He even had a joke to share with the crowd. He was not good at jokes, but would give it a try.

"Many of you will have seen the superbly original Fosdyke Challenger that has been on display all afternoon, so it will be no surprise when I ask the proud owner to join me to receive his well-deserved award."

"Ladies and gentleman, please give a big round of applause for…"

Toby got up from his seat and began to make his way forward.

"… all the way from Australia, Mr Bruce Adelaide."

Toby didn't hear the huge round of applause. He stared with disbelief as a nonchalant young chap in jeans and a rude T-shirt mounted the rostrum steps. Nonchalantly tucking the trophy under his arm, he shook hands with the President, waved to the crowd and was gone.

Toby pushed through the crowd towards the young Australian, catching him by the arm.

"Where is it?"

"Where's what?"

"Your bike! You say you have a Fosdyke, there are only three in the world and I know them all."

"You don't know this one, sport. My old dad restored it back home in Cairns. When he died he left it to me. Bloody old thing, I prefer my Kawasaki, but I brought it over, thought I could sell it. Might pay for a little apartment somewhere."

Toby wasn't listening as he stared at the world's fourth Fosdyke Challenger. It was a good restoration, but no, on careful examination, it was not as good as his.

The Australian seemed to read his mind.

"I saw yours, sport, lovely work, but I had to point out to the judges your bike just isn't original."

Not original, not original. The words were like a knife to Toby's heart. Twenty years of research. He was the world authority on all things Fosdyke.

"Yours is the 1922 TT model, yes I agree with that, the engine and frame numbers are right, but you've got the 1924 rear wheel with the reinforced hub splines. No hard feelings, mate. Come on, I'll buy you a pint before I ride home."

Once again, Toby wasn't listening. Running back to his van, he stared at his volumes of research notes, the old photographs, the original road tests. There was no doubt. His 1922 TT special had the 1924 rear wheel. How could he possibly have missed this obvious fact in twenty years of dedicated study?

Bruce Adelaide returned to his award-winning Fosdyke. Putting on his modern helmet, he went through the complicated starting procedure, watched by an appreciative crowd of enthusiasts. With a wave he was off and was soon speeding along the country lane leading away from the rally field.

The old bike was a bugger to ride at the best of times, but at near its maximum speed of sixty miles an hour, Bruce was finding it almost impossible to control. Something was wrong; it had never been this bad before. Fighting with the steering, he veered all over the road. The single front brake, ineffectual at the best of times, was hopeless in slowing the old racer.

Trying to hold the speeding museum exhibit on a hairpin bend, the ancient tyres gave up their grip and the machine and rider left the road, hit a tree and were catapulted into the deep roadside ditch.

Toby Reynolds stopped his Transit van and hurried across the road. Sliding down into the ditch, Toby dragged the groaning Bruce Adelaide from his ancient bike. Then, quickly unbolting the already loosened rear axle nuts, he pulled the 1922 rear wheel free of the wrecked machine, before scrambling back up to the road. Toby could smell the petrol as it poured from the upturned tank, soaking the Australian's clothes.

Placing the treasured wheel in the back of his van, he bowled his own 1924 wheel into the ditch, then returning to the cab he drove away, but not before flicking a lit cigarette end out of the window.

Glancing in his wing mirror, he could see the flames and smoke leaping from the funeral pyre.

He was satisfied, once again there were only three Fosdyke Challengers in existence and his would be perfect, with the correct 1922 rear wheel.

Neptune's Grasp

Colin Wyatt

Cold. Clear. Crystal cut.
Icy tongues of turbulent tide.
Thunderous sea, fathoms deep
Swept me to the Devil's side.
Weightless in this salty bath,
Eyes aflame, lungs denied.
With seaweed for an epitaph,
Engulfed, I clawed, and died.

100 Worder: **Drowsy**

Paul Westgate

Drowsy.

What a delightful word.

Suggesting the essence of long, lazy, hot summer days. Of gently humming bees. Of colourful flowers. Of a fountain tinkling. Of strawberries and cream. Of drifting far away. Of time pleasantly passing. Of peace and quiet contemplation. Of just five more minutes.

From the dictionary: adjective – half asleep, lulling, soporific.

From experience: a state of being.

Heavy head and leaden limbs pressed against soft cushions on a warm afternoon. Cares, not forgotten, but side-lined.

Life made bearable.

Two, three times a day.

Caution, may cause drowsiness, do not operate heavy machinery.

Bring it on!

Legion of One

Adam Isherwood

The Planet Kreuvaar
3,836.14.3 Years After Exodus

He felt the crushing impact to his left cranial plate.

Time slowed as his skull case shattered. With each microscopic explosion his nervous system shut down, one synapse at a time. He could leave this body at any moment but throughout his centuries of *"life"* – it was these moments of death that made him feel so alive. He wanted to savour every cold, dark sensation. The feeling of falling away into an all-encompassing abyss was nothing short of intoxicating but his bliss was cut short, safety protocols kicked in and he felt the sudden tug of his soul being shunted into another body.

Death could not touch him, for he was a Remnant of Earth, a digital preservation of a human soul that sacrificed itself for the protection of mankind's only hope: The Ark Fleet and its quest for a new home world for mankind.

As he awoke in the gun metal, angled plate frame of a new legionnaire drone, mere feet from the previous one, he watched his former self lifelessly cascade to the ground. He watched its cracked, half-moon ruin of a face leer at him as it greedily savoured those last sensations of finality that he could only imagine and yearn for.

The rejection seared his soul into rage as his gaze turned to his killer; a nine feet tall slab of muscle and scales, wrapped in the form of a monstrous simian, the indigenous of this world, the Kremuht. It swung its man-sized ornate stone mace in wide, wild figure-of-eight arches; with each

46

sweep he could see more of his drones being swept aside and sent reeling like rag dolls. Each one of the hundreds of drones that fought upon the battlefield were under his control, and in the back of his mind, with each drone's destruction, he could feel them shutting down, he envied them being granted the gift of death.

The Kreumuht were trying to break his legion's hold on an ancient temple, where beneath it was a natural reservoir of a liquid salt compound that made an excellent coolant for the Ark Fleet. As a general of the Sollun Conglomerate Security Forces, he was charged to hold this asset within all reasonable costs from the fanatical Kreumuht who worshipped their planet as a deity and perceived the salt compound as 'God blood'.

The mundane tedium of this battle bored him, this creature which failed to satisfy him bored him. He remembered when he was flesh and blood, when war was conducted under the tyranny of bullets and boots, when the fear of death kept the cost of blood in check. Now war was eternal and governed by digits and its only cost was the replacement of drones needed to reinforce each cohort. He became a Remnant to fight for mankind's survival, not a killer who conquered in the pursuit of engine maintenance. Like many of his kind, the years of existing within machines had taken its toll on his humanity. Sentiment eroded into logic, empathy into efficiency. He desired greatly a release from this presentiment of a manufactured extinction.

He tightened his grip on his gladius and shield and casually approached the beast. Like the ghost he had become, he drifted through the battle around him. His target did not notice him as it was preoccupied in pulling a drone apart like a wish bone. It thought the drones weak, the fool, it did not understand what it faced. Each drone was him and he was Legion. He approached it and without a shred of moral hesitation he plunged his gladius into the side of its neck, intentionally serrating just enough of the cerebrum to begin the chain reaction of its demise. He did not want it to die instantly, he did not want it to miss out on its one chance to taste bliss. As the light dimmed in its simple eyes, it looked at him, its messenger of death, he leaned his impassive steel face towards the beast and from the vox speaker behind his slit mouth he spoke:

"My gift to you."

Limerickish

Peter Sandling

Poor Wendall Sprog
Resembled a frog
So in life his outlook was sad
But then he met Lily
Who said 'don't be silly'
Come and live with me in my pad.

Repressed Leonard Prude
Could never be rude
It was something one just didn't do
But then he met Crystal
A transvestite from Bristol
And his life became explicit in Crewe.

Trickety Clack

Dave Traer

The two smartly dressed women struggled to pull their overfilled cases along the narrow corridor, hoping to find an empty compartment.

"This is ridiculous, I told you to grab that porter. You just don't realise how bad my back can get."

"Stop moaning, Ethel. If we'd waited for him to offload that trolley, we'd have lost any hope of getting a compartment to ourselves. Here, this one's empty." She slid open the door and sniffed. "It's clean as well. Get yourself sat by the window, while I drag the luggage in."

A plume of smoke drifted through the small open window.

Ethel grasped the clasp and tried to push it shut. "God, I hate these bloody trains. That smell of smoke, oil and steam gets everywhere. In your clothes, hair, skin. Every bloody where. And I can't close this bloody window."

"Sit down out of the way. Let me... See you only have to jiggle it a bit."

"Thank you. Now wave these fumes away, shut the door and leave the cases in front of it. They might help keep the riffraff out."

Jane did as her companion ordered before taking up residence in the seat opposite. The platform had disappeared in a cloud of white smoke.

"See, admit it, it's horrid."

"Are you going to spend the whole journey complaining? If you are, I'll go and find myself another compartment."

"But look, it's like the middle of the night out there."

Jane made to stand up.

"All right, stop getting all shirty with me. I'm sure I'll feel better once we get moving."

A whistle sounded and the comforting chug-chug of the engine pulled the carriages away from the station.

The compartment door opened with a bang. The startled pair watched in horror as a rather tall, overweight gentleman stumbled over their packed possessions. In an effort to save himself, he hopelessly threw his arms out. His small case refusing to help pulled one hand to the floor, while the other desperately tried to grab hold of something. It found Ethel's knee.

Jane didn't know whether her friend's scream was one of pain or shock, but it made her laugh. It was a nervous laugh, but Ethel was in no mood to tell the difference.

"How dare you sit there and snigger. Get this oaf off of me."

The man quickly moved the offending hand onto the adjacent seat and pulled himself erect.

Jane looked up at his bright red face. "Are you alright?"

"What are you asking him for? It's me he assaulted!"

She ignored the comment and watched as the man struggled into a seat.

"Are you okay?" she repeated.

"I think so. Nothing's broken, other than a little pride." His voice was soft and friendly. He turned to Ethel. "I'm ever so sorry. I didn't expect to walk into two heavy suitcases. I just saw the empty seats. Did I hurt your knee?"

She turned away from them both and glared out at the dwindling suburbs.

"She's alright, ignore her." Jane tried to rescue his case from the floor but gave up when she felt the weight of it.

"Don't even try to lift that, my dear." He stooped down and swung it onto the seat beside him. He held out his hand. "Clarence Fairweather."

51

Jane took it. "Jane. Jane Watson and this is my friend Ethel Turner."

"Pleased to meet you both."

Ethel huffed and stayed focussed on the green fields.

"How far are you going, if you don't mind me asking?"

Ethel turned from the window. "That's no concern of yours, young man."

"Sorry, I didn't mean to offend. I'm off to Edinburgh, for the festival."

"To spectate or perform?" Ethel asked, her interest suddenly aroused.

"A bit of both, I hope. I'm a magician."

"Oh, how thrilling. I do love magic," Jane cried. "Absolutely love it. Could you make Ethel disappear?"

"Now there's a mission," Clarence laughed. "Do you dislike her that much?"

"Only when she's like this. Which is most of the time."

"I am here you know," Ethel interjected. "Sometimes, Jane you can be so rude."

"That makes two of us then."

Ethel, red-faced, turned to the window.

"Can you do some magic for us? Get me to pick a card or something?" asked Jane.

"You can choose any trick you like. Take something from my case."

"What, anything?"

"Anything at all. Here…" He handed her a small key.

Ethel's curiosity got the better of her as her friend excitedly unlocked the case and plunged her arm into it.

"It's empty, totally empty." She lifted the open case, turned it over and shook it. "The only thing inside is air. But that's not possible. A minute ago I couldn't even lift it."

"No, that can't be right," Clarence complained. "Come out of the way and let me look."

He rolled up his sleeve and lowered in his hand. "Ah, here's something," he shouted as he lifted out an extremely large white rabbit.

The two women stared in disbelief.

"How the devil did you do that?" Ethel shouted.

"What this?" he replied, as he pulled out another one. "Now, what shall I do with these?"

"Are there any more in there?" Jane enquired.

"Possibly, you know what rabbits are like. There could be a whole new litter in there." He offered the two rabbits to Ethel. "Here hold on to these, while I take a look."

"Get those filthy things away from me," she shrieked as the compartment door slid open.

"Tickets please," the short, balding inspector bellowed, as he slid open the door. He stopped in his tracks. "Now then, you can't leave these cases there. That's what the luggage racks are for. If you can't lift them up I'll have to summon a porter to stow them in the baggage car. Show me your tickets first, then I'll get him."

As the three searched their pockets, the official's nose started to twitch. "Have you got livestock in here?"

"Livestock?" queried Clarence. "Of course not, Inspector. Just what you see. Two pieces of very heavy luggage and this small empty case. Oh, and us of course. Perhaps we just passed a farm."

The inspector knelt down and peered under the seats. "Maybe, but I can definitely smell something."

"You must have an overactive imagination," the magician suggested.

The inspector huffed his way back along the corridor.

"Where on earth did the rabbits go?" Jane laughed.

"Rabbits?" asked Clarence. "What rabbits?"

"Priceless," screamed Jane. "Absolutely priceless."

"It was a good job I didn't pull out Harold!" laughed the conjurer.

"Harold?" chuckled Jane.

"Let's see if I can find him." He reached into his case and lifted out the head of a huge bleating goat. "Hello old chap, say hello to my new friend."

Jane's laughter became hysterical. She rolled in her seat, holding her stomach. Her sides, her face, even her teeth ached. Waterfalls of tears flowed down her cheeks. Try as she might, she couldn't control herself.

Ethel's merriment, which started with a tentative giggle, quickly rose to Jane's level.

The conjurer smiled as he relocked his case.

It was a full ten minutes before Ethel realised that apart from herself and one very overweight suitcase, the compartment was completely empty.

She stood and rubbed the tears from her cheeks. The carriage was spotless. There were no indents in the seats, no mess on the floor. Just her and one lonely suitcase. Thinking it must have all been some kind of crazy dream, she wondered if Jane had come with her at all. Perhaps she just accompanied her to the station. Perhaps she was losing her mind.

The door slid open, and a porter lifted her case.

"Just putting this in the baggage car for you, Madam. Inspector's orders. He told me there were two cases. I guess he was mistaken."

Ethel watched as porter and case travelled along the corridor, leaving a trail of white fur in their wake.

Poem 1

Tracey Phillips

The way I think, is in black and white,
It's either wrong or it is right.
My brain is wired different to some,
People think I'm stupid, call me dumb.
I get so frustrated. Some say I'm bad.
I shout out. I know I'm loud.
I cry, I stamp, sometimes I swear.
I'm not even conscious of who is there.
I'm clever you know. Really, it's true!
There is so much that I can carefully do.
All I am asking, is see past the label,
I have Asperger's, and I am able.

Lady in Blue

Julie Kendall

I sit here texting on my phone
When I realise I am not alone.
A lady in blue sits next to me
With orange hair for all to see

Try not to stare it would be rude.
From her bag she produces food:
Big sandwich and a can of beer.
I wish I was not quite so near.

Up she gets from eating lunch,
Bunch of grapes still to munch
A man comes over to the seat
I note he has enormous feet.

A grey mac and a curly beard,
I think he looks rather weird.
Lady speaks and smiles at him
Hello, love, where you been?

I move along to give them room,
Really I need to leave here soon.
Can't help but listen to their chat,
They start to kiss, well fancy that!

He says, "I have the afternoon free."
They kiss again for all to see
Where shall we go? It's up to you.
Shall we get a bus to the zoo?

I want to sit and listen more
But my jaw drops to the floor.
With Hairy legs and hairy hand
This lady in blue is really a man!

Graffiti

Debz Hobbs-Wyatt

The edges are blurred, the lines between dark and light ill-defined as if they're folded together.

I watch a raindrop cross a dirty window, stare across grey rooftops, and I think how I hate Thursdays.

The world ended on a Thursday.

It's easy to stare at nothing for too long. The randomness of lists on a fridge door: baked beans crossed off, shampoo underlined, the name of a play by an unknown writer we heard on Radio 4, and a magnetic memento of a day trip to Brighton when there were day trips to Brighton. It holds a photograph of you, aged fifteen. You can't tell. You look like any normal kid.

No one ever knows how things will turn out.

Morning news claims rising costs of living and layoffs at factories. I picture Dad, proud in a neon vest and hard hat, reminiscences of his *Health and Safety Days*: the officer, the enforcer. Life defined by punching a time-clock. But look where it got him. Or didn't get him.

"A good honest living," he said. "None of that artsy fartsy nonsense."

Of course he meant me, not you.

"You think you'll make a living ACTING?" he said, his doubt booming across a newly fitted kitchen while Mum stirred stew with a wooden spoon and looked the other way. "Look at your brother, going to the polytechnic. A vocation is what you need. People always need civil engineers."

You tried to tell him they always need actors too and what would he do without Bond – James Bond – on wet bank holiday Mondays? But all he did was laugh. You always made him laugh.

And the whole time Mum said nothing. You said some people keep things on the inside, because they don't know how to say them.

I can still see our house in West Hampstead where we grew up, you and I. Mum would turn in her grave if she heard me: You and me. *ME* not I. What did she think would happen if I used the wrong word, did she think the world would end?

I picture our house, with its enduring scent of lemon polish. A brick fireplace where shiny porcelain shire horses pulled invisible carts. The Top Forty countdown on Sunday nights, all of us singing along to Brotherhood of Man, and Auntie Shelly saving all her kisses for outstayed welcomes because Dad made the mistake of boasting about having a spare room. *And* a car port.

What do I have?

Cups stained with the entrails of too much tea; splashes of milk spilled from recyclable plastic that I won't recycle; toast crumbs scooped into a grey dishcloth moulded with the shape of my hand and chip fat splashes scarring the surface of a metal hob.

But it's home. And at least I didn't desert you when you needed me.

Sometimes I wonder where that place went. I imagine it's behind a closed door that one day I'll find, quite by chance. Maybe in Debenhams: a wrong door in the fitting rooms. And there you'll be, as if you've always been there, and our lives have been playing out in parallel the whole time. Mum still baking butterfly cakes that she wheels out on a hostess trolley, Dad laughing at you doing those rancid impressions of David Bellamy while uprooting Mum's rubber plant.

59

I think about that as I stand at the window, counting the lives on the other side where new memories are spun. You just never realise how fragile all the threads are.

I'm still staring too long at nothing. Thinking that rooftops wear metal crowns like thorns, and further up the hill, big shiny dishes. But it's all the same: people tuning into the same pulse. A place where it's hard to see the line between fiction and reality. For some it's the first thing they do in the morning, reach for a button just to hear someone speak.

London hides beneath her mantle of greyness, rain darts sideways across glass and I wait for a kettle to boil, for something to happen, for the day to end. Thursday will turn into Friday, the way a butterfly emerges from its chrysalis. And it's not just any Friday, month-end Friday where holes in walls spew out their paper. It's a miracle of urban living. Paper turned into wine.

Or worse.

As I walk from the skinny kitchen into the living room, the flat rattles, ripples dance across tea, as the 16.50 northbound train takes people into the city. I think of all the times I was one of them: neon words flashing past, urban messages without bottles.

Looking for you.

"Remember the emotion; draw upon it." It's what Robert said. Robert Frazier Pugh, Head of Performing Arts with his smile and *his way*. He said it the day I told him about you. I was a second year on an *artsy fartsy* course, living on air and dreams because someone said you didn't need anything else, while you, Dad's perfect blue-eyed boy, was folded over like a comma on my bathroom floor; skinny, destitute, DESPERATE, begging me to help you feel normal.

I had no one else to turn to. How could I tell Dad the real reason you dropped out of the polytechnic had nothing to do with 'pursuing alternative career options'.

They tell me Robert Frazier Pugh bedded a lot of his students, but *I* was different. He was going to leave his wife for me, pay for you to go to The Priory. Amazing what you believe in a three star London hotel room in a champagne haze, promises forced out in breathy stutters as your head is pounded against a headboard; flesh grinding against flesh.

You always said he was no good.

In the reflection of the silent TV I see Mum's face in mine. When they first found out about you, they told friends you were sick, in a hospital *out of town*. And people would say how wonderfully they both soldiered on. But the only difference was Mum's pills came with a note from a doctor who didn't even look up when he handed it over. And Dad pissed his into a toilet pan, along with what was left of his meagre redundancy.

They would later recount their tales of woe, then too large to brush under carpets, about how they tried *so* hard to help you. But anyone can see that one chance, one cash handout for a rehab program was destined to fail.

But I don't blame them.

They did enough of that for themselves.

They say the world can change in a blink, like watching a line turn blue on a stick, two weeks after the man who was going to leave his wife for you, left *you* instead. And all this at the same time YOU, my crazy brother, were leaving messages on garage doors and writing poetry about despair on derelict buildings. You told me there was no point in living at the same time I told you I carried a life inside me.

61

You taught me to believe in happy ever after. Something *you* never believed in.

But some outcomes are inevitable.

I reach for the plate balanced next to the tea cup. The day is edged with peanut butter, sometimes I think it's the only thing that holds the pieces together. You loved peanut butter.

17.46, the southbound train. Clinkedy clink. I stare too long at the window; net curtains drape another layer of greyness between me and the orange glow of street lamps that bleed into the drizzle.

You were the only one that knew about Robert. You were living with me at that time, promising that *this was it. You would do it this time, pay back every penny you stole.* I guess it's not a lie if you believe it when you say it.

And by then Dad had stopped talking to me too. I tried to imagine what he'd say if he knew I was scribbling lists of '*whys*' and '*why nots*' for having his illegitimate grandchild swathed in yellow plastic stamped CLINICAL WASTE.

As if all our mistakes end up in the same place.

18.10 northbound, fast train. Nystagmic eyes flick across words sprayed onto walls. Streaks of colour seen only by those that care to seek them. I remember when you tried to explain how they were the modern postcard, a place for self-expression.

"That's what the therapy was supposed to be for," I told you. But all you did was shrug.

"It's about finding a voice," you said. "An identity, like a signature that marks out territory."

I liked the primeval simplicity of what you said. And one day I came home to find you working on your identity:

the initials of your name woven together, DJP (Dylan James Pinter) scribbled repeatedly on scraps of paper, the edges of the D tapered at the corner. I watched you, your jaw pushed forward the way you always did when you were deep in concentration. You wrote the same three letters over and over until they were perfect, until you had them right.

When you left they were the same letters I sought as I turned every corner. As if London was a giant billboard, words smeared across a landscape, the voices of the unseen. And all I needed were three letters, a D tapering at the corner in fresh paint. It was the only way I knew you were still alive.

You came back to me once. Stood in the doorway, clothes sliding off what was left of you, legs twitching as if your demons had finally reached the outside. I think that's when I knew. I was looking into eyes with no reflection, searching for the face of a little boy that did David Bellamy impressions and threw his head back when he laughed. But he was behind a door somewhere, in a parallel universe.

I begged you to stay. But I always knew you wouldn't.

18.46 southbound, slow train. Clinkedy clink. I pull the curtain across, peer at the wetness on the street below. It won't be long now.

After you left, I walked the London streets, looked for you in parks and on bus shelters. When I found you I wept with relief, but then it stopped. As if the paint had run out. And now I could only see where you'd been, and not where you were.

I suppose that's when I really knew. But still I searched, rode the train to Brighton, hoping.

And then it happened. THE phone call; when a random Thursday morning stopped being random. Me, standing in a towel, still holding the telephone long after it disconnected, as if time had stopped.

For a long time, the letters that replaced yours were 'O.D.' That's what the coroner said. I imagined it with the D tapering at the corner.

19.25, all stops northbound. I stand at the window and watch two figures turn the corner. Dad looks up, lifts his hand; beside him, your nephew, football boots in a Tesco carrier bag, handsome as you were at fifteen.

I never told Dad how you talked me out of going to the clinic that day. Or that sometimes I imagine an alternative universe, one without Freddy "Dylan" Pinter. But it's a door I'll never open.

I hear their footsteps on the stairs. Dad sits with Freddy most nights. He doesn't need to but I think it's his way of making up for something.

So I'll take the 20.01 northbound, four stops to the little theatre on Halfpenny Lane. I don't come on until the third act, it's only a small part. But it's enough. We all need to find our identity.

And on the train I look for you. 'DJP', the D tapering at the corner.

Busy Life

Peter Sandling

It seems that with the rush and tear
Life pulls you down, too much to bear
But step back once and once again
And see another time, less strain.
Be thankful for the gift of life
With all its beauty, not its strife
To marvel at a drop of rain
A sunset never seen again.
The flowering tree, the wind so fair
With blossom falling in your hair.
See ripples running in a stream,
The shafts of sunlight in a beam.
I'd like to always think of these,
Reflect on life, just at my ease.
But life's to live, and this is mine
I hope my train's on time.

No Clichés Please!

Colin Wyatt

Derek Morris looked at his watch and noted that in five minutes' time the bell would be sounding to denote the end of the day's lessons.

He glanced around the classroom at the twenty-six pupils to whom he had been attempting to teach English Language. Morris felt rather smug. He had a very high opinion of himself, and thought his pupils and the school were very lucky to have him. He was in no doubt that there was no one better suited than himself to pass on the superior knowledge he had gained after almost forty years of teaching. Whether the pupils wanted to share that superior knowledge was another matter.

Unfortunately most of them didn't!

Derek Morris was happily unaware of that fact. Even had he been aware he would have found it impossible to believe. Morris was a supremely confident man. He was confident that he was respected as a teacher. Had he known what his fourteen-year-old pupils, and some of the staff, said about him behind his back, he may not have been so confident. But confidence was what Derek Morris had in abundance. How could he be anything else, when his judgement was so impeccable that he was never *ever* wrong? Not in his opinion anyway. This was something that not only annoyed his pupils but also his wife, Diane. That was another thing that Morris was unaware of!

Morris was spending this last lesson of the day on his favourite subject. The thing he felt most passionate about: the use of superfluous language in every day speech and the written word. "There are far too many clichés and

66

exaggerations used," Morris said passionately. "It's totally unnecessary and therefore quite wrong." He paused for some effect. "You would certainly never hear me using them!"

A hand shot up. This was Rupert Davis. He was one of Morris's brightest pupils. But he was also one of his most exasperating. Davis had an annoying way of testing Morris's patience to its utmost limits.

"Yes Davis?" said Morris testily.

"I'm sure you must have used some, Sir," said Davis. "Everyone does!" He glanced around at his classmates and gave a little wink. "Perhaps you could give us some examples, Sir? So that we know what we should be saying and what we shouldn't."

Derek Morris was quite sure Davis could have thought of some himself and this was just his way of wasting time. Morris breathed deeply. "Very well," he said. "For instance there is, 'I've told you a million times!' Or, 'I could eat a horse!' Neither could be true, of course."

This caused a ripple of amusement around the classroom.

"And of course," he went on, "there are clichés like, 'it's as long as a piece of string'!"

"What would you say instead of that, Sir?" called Davis without putting up his hand.

Morris stared at Davis for a moment. "I would say," he said loudly, "that the thing is 'eight inches long' or 'ten inches long'. Whatever the correct size might be!"

"I bet either would make Mrs Morris happy!" Rupert Davis said.

A roar of laughter erupted around the classroom.

Derek Morris's face was scarlet. "Davis! You impertinent young devil!" he said, striding across the classroom towards him. "I'll see you get detention for this!"

"Detention, Sir! But why, Sir? I just meant that surely

Mrs Morris would be happy to know that you're using the language properly. What did you think I meant?"

Derek Morris turned his back on the class and returned to his desk. He breathed in deeply for several seconds to regain his composure. He was annoyed with himself that this was another instance of him allowing Davis to 'wind him up'! With some difficulty Morris stayed calm. He was, after all, a teacher with some integrity. He would retain his dignity. He glanced down at his watch. It was almost time for the bell.

"Right boys!" he said at last. "For your homework today I want you to write a list of clichés and exaggerations used in every day speech, and that you may have read. Then give alternative explanations for them." He glanced around at his class. "You can use the examples I've mentioned but think of as many more as you can…" Morris was interrupted by the sound of the bell.

"Right boys!" he said again with some relief. "Put away your books and you may go!"

"Whatever is troubling you Derek?" Diane Morris asked her husband that question as they sat at their table eating dinner. "You've hardly said a word, and I can see by your face that something's up!"

Derek Morris chewed on some meat for a few moments before swallowing it. "It… it's that boy Davis. I've mentioned him before. He just gets me so worked up!"

His wife raised her eyebrows. "Worked up!" It had been a long time since she had heard that expression in connection with her husband. After nearly thirty-five years of marriage he still managed to surprise her. But not in that way!

Diane quickly dismissed the thought. She shook her head slowly. "You're a grown man, Derek. You're his teacher! Why on earth do you let him do it?"

Morris knew that his wife was right but he still felt

frustrated. "I don't think he respects me, and I can't think why. I'm sure the other boys do! He is constantly trying to undermine me, even though I'm always right!"

Mrs Morris looked at her husband but said nothing. "You know that's true dear, of course!" added Morris.

Diane Morris put a forkful of food in her mouth so that she didn't have to answer.

"Do you know," went on Morris, "he actually had the cheek to imply that I used clichés. Just like other people!"

Diane Morris looked across at her husband. "Whatever next!" she said, trying to hide a smile. "I hope you're going to have him expelled for that!"

Morris didn't see the joke. "I'm being serious Diane! How dare he?"

Morris and his wife finished eating their dinner in silence.

"I'll take Rosie for her walk," Morris said at last, rising from the table. Rosie was their black and white cocker spaniel, and he always took her out in the evening. Diane Morris glanced out of the window. "I don't think Rosie will want to go. It's peeing down with rain."

"Diane!" snapped Morris. "Don't say things like that. You know I don't like it!"

Diane Morris looked around at her husband. "What's wrong with saying 'peeing'? I could have said something a lot worse!"

Morris pulled the curtain aside and glanced out at the rain. He turned to his wife and frowned. "You could have said, "IT'S RAINING CATS AND DOGS!"

There was a moment of silence as both Morris and his wife realised the impact of what he just said.

Then there was a burst of laughter from Diane Morris. BUT SHE DIDN'T SAY A WORD!

Dedication: Thanks to my wife, Jan, for her love and encouragement.

Limerickish

Peter Sandling

Shy Millicent Pucket
Lived in a bucket
And rarely received any mail
This upset her wellbeing
So her friends started seeing
Poor Millie becoming a little pail.

Sly Myrtle Pillick
Ran a liposuction clinic
Her unique business skills demanded more
She disposed of the fat
Not by storing in a vat
But through pipework to the chippy next door.

The Perfectionist

Margaret Potter

There were three of us in the flat. Old Ma Baker with her precious doll. Funny looking thing, face screwed up like a newborn ready to cry.

Old Ma Baker nursed that damn thing from morn until night, and the day Ray found an old pram on the tip, you would think she had won a million pounds.

Ray pushed that pram all the way from Elston tip to number 5 Gordon Street.

He said, "Here you are Ma."

She squealed in delight and fished inside her box of precious things, bringing out a rainbow-coloured blanket to lie in the pram.

She would shoogle that thing for hours. We even had to remind her to eat.

I said, "Come on Ma, have your soup or that there babe of yours will end up an orphan."

She'd eat then, a distant look in her faded blue eyes.

I've been at number 5 Gordon Street for nigh on six months now. It's not what I would call perfect, not in my eyes any road, but it's clean and dry.

Ma Baker said I should give over sweeping and dusting. She said all that moving about was bad for her chest, and me on the go all the time was bad for her peace of mind.

I told her straight, "Cleaning and polishing is what keeps me sane."

Ray is a big help. He's always coming back with stuff for my cleaning regime. Oh, he doesn't thieve it, he finds it. He reckons we are a throw-away society.

I said, "Thems that have, throw away. I don't throw away."

Then I go into my room to look at my sparse possessions all neatly lined up in rows, and woe betide anyone who moves them.

Ray says I can be a right firecracker when I get going. Says I'm worse than some of the clientele he's met in the nick. Then he laughs showing two missing front teeth.

I said, "My firecracker temper has kept me alive."

I don't say how. Some of that stuff I keep buried.

I told him straight, "I ain't dredging all that up for no one."

He don't press me. He reckons he's got his own demons to fight.

Ma Baker looks up and says quietly, "We all have."

Then a single tear makes a clean track down her grubby cheek.

Man from the council's been again. Ray was all for not letting him in. For all his bravado, he's scared stiff of authority. If he sees a clipboard he disappears.

I said, "I'm not afraid."

The council chap gives the flat the once over. Reckons the electrics are well dodgy and writes notes.

He said, "You are a fire hazard. There has been a complaint."

I said, "It'll be that stuck up cow from number 6. She's always poking her nose in our business."

He reckoned he wasn't at liberty to say but if we don't comply, we'll be hearing from him again.

When he's gone Ray comes out of his room.

He says, "No problem. My mate, Slippery Joe, has done time for hot wiring; what he don't know about electrics isn't worth knowing."

I get my duster out again and give the table a good rub and round the brass on the fire. I catch a glimpse of myself. Ugly scarred face stares back at me and I can hear the battle cries again and see the carnage left behind.

Ray puts a steadying hand on my shoulder and the shaking stops. His voice gruff and soft in my ear.

"Come on Lily, I've made a brew."

"Sgt Lillian Mathews reporting for duty, Sir."

I see myself saluting smartly and hear the clip of my heels. The commanding officer is giving us the run down of proceedings. I can feel the pride swell in my chest as I listen to his words.

"We strive for perfection. We are perfection."

The photo on Mum's mantelpiece flashes before me. Smart army uniform, bright eager eyes and a smile radiating across my unblemished face.

"Ray, this tea is too hot."

I put it down for later as any hot liquid aggravates. Ray says he's off out to find his electrical contact, alias Slippery Joe, on account of his expertise at slipping police cordons.

Old Ma Baker nods off and for once the pram sits idle. I take my duster out and polish all the ornaments again. Habits are hard to break.

Ray's electrical mate arrives and Ray announces he'll work for tea and a piece of my delicious homemade sponge.

I give Slippery my best lopsided grin and watch as he swallows hard in response. I guess he's seen some things in his time but not perhaps a face like mine.

While I make the tea, the consultant's last conversation comes to mind.

"There isn't any more we can achieve, Miss Mathews.

We've saved your sight, which is tip-top. You must just get on with your life."

I leave feeling dismissed. The army for all its faults had arranged all my rehabilitation and my fiancé had been my strength. He had hidden his shock at seeing me and hidden his relief even better, when I told him it was over for us.

I could even laugh at his jokes.

He'd said, "Your modelling days are over, Lily, but you're still my perfect girl."

Only I wasn't perfect, was I?

When I take the tea in, Slippery Joe doesn't bat an eyelid. Instead he takes a bite of the sponge and winks. Old Ma Baker takes her babe and cradles it, crooning happily as she looks into its porcelain face.

As I sit amongst my flawed friends I say, "What is perfection?"

Then it comes to me in a wave of contentment. This, here and now, is perfection.

Being Human

Phil Horscroft

My soul is in darkness, my heart lost in pain
As I realise I've let God down again.
The people around me all say "I'm impressed"
But God, who knows better, I'm sure I've distressed.
When will I learn to master my greed?
When will I see I have all I need?
I cannot forgive my thoughtless misdeeds.
I cannot pull up all my wildly sewn weeds.
I tell God "I'm sorry" for causing Him pain.
I tell God "I'm sorry," but I'll do it again.
I beg for forgiveness and mercy for me.
I beg for a place in eternity.
I beg Him for strength to turn from my sin.
I beg "Get me out from the mess that I'm in."
I'm talking to God, I know that He's there.
I know that He's listening, I'm sure of His care
The answer I'm given is simple and clear.
The answer I'm given reduces my fear.
"Don't stare at the bad things, remember the good.
Step back from yourself, see the trees *and* the wood.
Everyone sins, no-one's perfect, you see.
The way that God made you is the way you must be.
To do good or bad is the choice you must make.
To care and repair, or be thoughtless and break.
Don't judge yourself, for that's not your place
Don't judge your friends or the whole human race.
Just do what you can to stay free from sin.
Just follow God's plan from the mess that you're in.
One step at a time, that's the best you can do
And each step you take God will be there with you."

The Watchers

Henry Lewi

It was the first time they'd been back to Amsterdam for twenty years.

They had met when they were post-grad students at the Free University, Guy was doing post-doctoral research on the wartime diamond trade between the Netherlands and Nazi Germany and she was doing her PhD in International Law. His doctoral thesis titled *Nazis, Diamonds and the Post-War resurgence of Right Wing Extremism* had been well received.

For both it was love at first sight and as soon as Therese had received her doctorate, they had married in Amsterdam. His doctorate opened many academic doors, and from Amsterdam they had moved to London for five years where he had been a lecturer in War Studies at Kings College whilst Therese had worked at one of the American banks in London. London was followed by time at New York, Harvard and finally as Chairman of the Department of Conflict and Holocaust Studies, and Director of the Hoover Institute at Berkley, California. Therese likewise prospered and whilst they had lived in New York, had taken her Bar Exams and now in California was a partner in one of the Big Law firms specialising in International Banking Law.

The Archives of the Hoover Institute had been a treasure trove for his studies. He had published four books and numerous academic papers on the funding and rise of right wing extremist groups in Europe and their links with the illicit diamond trade, which had at its focal point, the movement of diamonds between Rio de Janiero and Amsterdam.

In January 2016 he was offered the invitation of

becoming the Erasmus Visiting Professor in Modern History back at the Free University in Amsterdam, and would present the opening address at the EU sponsored congress on 'European stability and the growing threat from Extremism'. It would be a great idea to both travel to Europe, especially as their twentieth wedding anniversary would occur the day before the conference was due to start.

They drove from their home overlooking San Pablo Bay to San Francisco Airport in his old white Porsche convertible, before taking the direct flight to Schiphol. On arrival, they were met as they disembarked by a member of the EU sponsoring commission, and were transported by a more sombre black Mercedes S500 to the 'Hotel American', that he had specifically requested. The newly refurbished hotel, which dated back to the 1930s, overlooked the Amstel, and was sited not far from the museums, diamond centre and the exclusive shopping streets of Amsterdam. The American Bar was claimed to be the best in the city and reputed to serve the finest Manhattans in Europe. The conference was due to commence two days after their arrival.

Their first day was spent reacquainting themselves with the sights and sounds of Amsterdam, hiring a couple of bikes and visiting some of the old coffee houses of the city. They were both amazed at the huge growth in the number of houseboats that had occurred in the last twenty years that now lined the canals. Many of these had been individually designed and were positively luxurious. In the evening, they were glad to see that the inhabitants of the city still continued with the habit of leaving their curtains and blinds wide open so passers-by could see directly into the living rooms.

That evening, the EU Commission had invited the conference speakers and their accompanying partners to a late dinner at the ultra-chic restaurant 'Le Garage', often frequented by celebrities, footballers and politicians. What they both noticed as they were driven around the square in front of the Museum Quarter was a strangely silent candlelight protest of about a thousand people, dressed in black and carrying banners denoting the Dutch right wing organisation, *'Democratische Organisatie van de Oostelijke Reich'* and surrounded by a similar number of silent riot police.

"I see the *DooR* are still making their presence felt," he said to the accompanying EU Commissioner, Edouard, "this whole right wing movement is spreading across Europe. Has this protest anything to do with the congress?"

"I'm afraid so," replied Edouard, "you'll see them all over Amsterdam, dressed in black, wearing their red armbands."

Dinner at Le Garage was a great success, the escargots were truly amazing and their main courses (pork for Therese and steak tartare for him) were the best they'd ever eaten. Leaving the restaurant, the guests almost walked into a dozen silent 'Watchers' gathered outside the restaurant, all dressed in black with their signature armbands. No words were exchanged, though he noted that three of them were watching him intently as they walked to their car, one even smiling and nodding at him. *Bloody strange*, he thought as they drove away.

The following day was spent at the Congress Centre, meeting EU representatives, chairing a pre-congress workshop and meeting members of Europol who had a specific remit in monitoring extremist political parties.

That evening, which marked their wedding anniversary, he had organised a private candlelight canal dinner cruise for the both of them, having arranged the exclusive private hire of the boat, chef and crew of three. The boat was waiting for them at the hotel's private jetty and as they boarded, Guy noted two of the black clad members of *DooR* watching them from just a few yards away. The table was set on the starboard side of the boat and Therese took her seat with her back to the bow whilst Guy faced forward. Her favourite aperitif of a Kir Royale was served to both of them (in truth he'd have preferred a whisky sour, but what the hell, it was her day as well he thought). Over the next two hours the chef served a truly remarkable seven course 'tasting menu', each dish served with a specially selected wine. The boat followed the one-way system imposed on the canal routes after dark. The canal-side was lit up, as were the many bridges, but he noted that on almost every bridge along their route stood two of the watchers, observing their leisurely progress. *Like a guard of honour,* Guy thought.

As they drank their coffee and sipped their cognacs, the boat slowly turned off the main canal and followed one of the smaller waterways. Intrigued, he glanced up and looked at a lit-up three storey canal-side building with six brightly lit full-length windows, two to each floor. Standing in each of the middle two windows stood a single figure, silhouetted by the bright light behind. The figures stood motionless, feet slightly apart and hands in their pockets clearly watching the progress of their boat. As the boat swung to the left following the route of the canal, he was able to look directly at the brightly lit scene, when suddenly the left hand figure staggered and fell forward as a dark cloud formed on the window in front and the figure slid to the ground. Within seconds they had moved on and he lost sight of the building.

"Fucking hell," he said to Therese, "did you see that?

"See what?" she said.

79

"I think I've just seen someone being shot back there," Guy said, getting up and going forward to the captain, "and there's no fucking signal," he said looking at his phone.

"Captain," he said, "I think there's been a shooting back there and we need to call the police, can we turn back?"

"I'm sorry, Professor, we can't turn around," replied the captain, "I'll bring the boat to a stop, and radio the police with our canal position. Are you sure of what you've seen?"

"Perfectly sure," Guy replied.

Within minutes a small police launch with its flashing blue lights appeared, and helped both Guy and Therese aboard and slowly backtracked the cruiser's canal route, until they reached the canal-side location of the building where Guy had seen the shooting, and as before, all six windows were lit up. The middle left window was partly obscured by a dark, irregular stain covering the middle third of the glass.

"This is it!" shouted Guy, as one of the policemen spoke to his colleagues on the radio.

"Okay," he said, "they've located and entered the apartment, and would like you and your wife to join them," he added, guiding the police launch to the canal-side.

The police escorted Guy and Therese to the large living room of the apartment on the middle floor. Police were grouped around a crumpled figure lying on the floor against the full-length window.

"Oh my God, it's Edouard!" exclaimed Therese,

"He's one of the EU Commissioners sponsoring our congress," explained Guy, "an expert on right wing extremism within the EU, and was going to give a paper on the *DooR* at the congress later today."

"Thank you, Professor," replied one of the police, "I'm Commissioner van Rijn and I'll be handling the investigation, but I think you were meant to have this." He reached into his inside pocket and handed over a slim white envelope with Guy's full title and name printed across the front.

Guy noted that the policeman had a red badge on his left lapel, on which, without his glasses, he thought he could make out the letters D-o-o-R embossed on it. Looking over the commissioner's shoulder and through the window, Guy could see a half dozen 'Watchers' standing together on the opposite side of the canal all looking up at the window.

Poem 2

Tracey Phillips

Am I the   only one?
It can't just   be me.......
who struggles to   put it on properly?
I twist it round,   and I do it up...
then lean each   one into a cup,
I jiggle about, pull the straps high,
then stand up with a sigh.
Think, thank God that's done,
now I'm all stressed,
I've put on my bra.
Now to get dressed...!

Dedicated to my Beautiful sister Kara. You will always be my inspiration.
XX

82

Sindy

Julie Kendall

You appear again today.

This time I'm in the bath and there you are with your long dark hair in a ponytail, beautiful eyes, smiling at me… yet you're not real, just my imagination, but to me you're so alive.

You're wearing blue again and as soon as you're there looking at me, I can relax. Maybe you're my imaginary friend, like Willow; she has one, but she's five and I'm forty. I want to stay here soaking in the bath, soaking you in, but if I tell Sally she'll think I'm losing the plot and laugh.

I've seen you over the last few weeks in numerous places; I was on a train going home from work and as I was dozing off I opened my eyes and there you were, smiling at me. I felt you mouthed the words 'Are you alright, Tom?' I find a lot of times when I see you I can't even try to answer, as I feel I am the only one that sees you.

The other day you entered my office; I didn't see the door open, but you were sitting opposite me. My phone rang and as I answered it, you were gone again.

Are you a ghost, Sindy?

I guess you must be.

I'm still daydreaming in the bath when Sally calls me, my lovely wife of six years. I love her so much; I just wish I could get Sindy to not intrude. "You wanted to watch that documentary, Tom," I hear her shout out.

"Soon be out, darling," I reply.

I get dressed and later we cuddle up on the settee after Sally has put Willow to bed.

"You can put her to bed tomorrow – oh and next

Thursday as I am out with Linda for a meal to celebrate her birthday."

I say okay and carry on watching the television with my arms wrapped round Sally.

"We don't go out on our own as much as we should, perhaps you could ask Linda if she will look after Willow one evening?" I say.

Sally agrees and says she'll ask her. That night as I am dropping off to sleep, Sindy appears again in my thoughts. I have given her the name Sindy as she reminds me of Willow's Sindy Doll but with dark hair.

As I'm walking to the office from Liverpool Street station, I see Sindy coming toward me; I feel I almost brush past her and when I look behind me, she isn't there.

I wonder if I should tell Sally what I've been experiencing, but she'll think I've gone slightly mad. I wonder if Sindy died in tragic circumstances. If she *is* a ghost I'm sure our cat Molly would sense the presence.

When I arrive home that evening I feel anxious and I don't really know why. I see a car pull away as I turn the corner into our road. Must be one of Sally's friends. As I walk into the lounge, Sally looks like she's been crying. I ask her if something's wrong and she says she was just getting tearful over a film on television. She seems really quiet and I decide not to mention Sindy. After all, it's just my imagination running away with me. Isn't it?

A few days later I come home to an empty house.

Sally didn't say she would be out tonight so where's Willow? Perhaps she's out with her friend, Linda?

I ring Sally but get no answer so I decide to call Linda. I have her number on my phone.

"Is Sally with you?"

"Err, no Tom, but she may be popping round later, I think. Willow is playing with Cynthia's daughter; I can see them from my kitchen window."

"Oh thanks, I'll come and get her."

I go to see Cynthia and as we're talking, Willow runs to the door. "Hi Daddy, Mummy dropped me here after school and I have had my tea here with Simone."

"Oh well, I wish Mummy had told me, but I have you now."

When Sally gets home she seems tired and not up to discussing anything. She just said "Oh well, you found where Willow was then Tom" then she went straight to bed.

I have started to feel uneasy; something's not right. I hope Sally's not lying to me. I watch her asleep next to me and my heart aches as I want things to be normal between us.

I'm feeling drowsy when I see Sindy again, at the bottom of our bed. She seems to say, "Are you okay, Tom?" and smiles at me. I want to grab her but I know it's just my imagination playing tricks on me again.

It becomes a regular night out with Linda: Sally tells me Linda is depressed after splitting with Geoff and needs cheering up. They go for meals, a show or just drinks, but always every week and she seems to have this excitement about her the day before.

I come home early one day the following week and the house is empty, but I guess Sally is most likely gossiping down the school or has gone for a coffee with one of the mums.

There is a ring at the door; Cynthia is standing there with Willow.

"Sorry, Tom, I was hoping you would be home early tonight as I need to go to collect something and it will be easier without Willow as it's a bit of a walk for her. Hope that's okay if she comes home now?"

"Yes of course. I just managed to get away early tonight as a meeting was cancelled. Where has Sally gone this time?"

"Lakeside I think," says Cynthia. I shut the door and start making Willow and me some tea. The phone rings and it's Sally.

"Sorry Tom, do you mind if we go to the pictures after shopping? A brilliant film's on."

I feel like saying, no it's not okay, I want you home, but I just say, "Yes if that's what you want."

I hear Sally close the front door at midnight that night. She creeps in and gets into bed beside me, I can smell aftershave but perhaps it's mine. As I try to cuddle her I feel her tense up and I feel close to tears.

The next day is a Saturday and Sally's mobile rings. She rushes to answer it and then takes the call in the kitchen. Later she's having a bath and I notice her mobile phone is still on the table. It rings so I go to answer it to tell her friend she is in the bath, but I hear a voice at the other end. It says, "Hi darling, can you talk? I miss you so much."

The phone feels like a lead weight in my hand and I put it down. In shock, I just sit there till Sally comes out of the bathroom.

"You had a call, Sally, it was a man; was it a wrong number? He asked if you could talk."

Sally just stares and I watch her face drain of colour and then she sobs.

"I am so sorry, Tom, I never meant to get involved but it just happened and I'm in love with him. I am so so sorry to hurt you like this."

My world is over, my life, my perfect happy family is in shreds. I walk out of the house and get in the car and I just drive, thinking, driving, tears burning my cheeks, then I don't remember anything else.

When I wake up my first thought is Sally.

Where is she, where am I?

I try to move my legs but I can't. I am floating and feeling numb and yet my body aches all over. I try to talk, to call out but nothing comes. *Where is this? Am I in a dream?* I can hear voices in the distance but my eyes keep closing again and I am back asleep. I feel I'm in between reality and dreams.

I can hear Sally's voice and she's crying, saying she's sorry, and then I remember. My Sally is seeing someone else and she loves him. I am heartbroken and I just close my eyes as I don't want to be here, I feel so numb.

A voice says that I have been in a serious road traffic accident; I gather it's a doctor, and I'm in hospital.

"You've been unconscious for a few days, you have a few fractures and your leg has been pinned. We also had to remove a finger as it was so badly crushed. Mr Hayes, you are lucky to still be here."

Lucky?

No. Unlucky. I don't want to be here, but then I think of Willow and realise I need to live for her, she needs her dad.

I must go off to sleep again, and for the next few days I am in and out of consciousness. I wake up and can see a lady standing over the bed. She is dressed in blue and has a lovely smile: a nurse, but there is something even stranger. She says, "Are you okay, Tom?" and I see it's Sindy, but this time she's real, and I give a little smile. "I'm Charlotte. You will be seeing a lot of me and we will get you better, Tom."

Poem 3

Tracey Phillips

What if...

      ... the dress don't fit,
      what will I truly do?

What if...

      ... my shoes are too tight,
      I've just one pair, not two.

What if...

      ... it pours with rain,
      and the roads are flooded deep?

What if...

      ... the alarm don't work,
      and through the day I sleep?

What if...

      ... the disco is crap
      and no one wants to dance?

What if...

      ... my man runs away,
      he don't want to take the chance.

What if...

      ... the registrar's sick,
      and we cannot get wed?

What if...

      ... the guests all revolt,
      and stay home, tucked up in bed?

But, I'm being positive – it will all be great,
because in a few days' time, I'll marry my best mate!

Glimpses of Hell

Peter Sandling

You open the door and step into the room. Your eyes slowly adjust to the low level lighting from the countless flickering candles as the patterns on the walls appear to reach out to you. Memories long forgotten force their way into your consciousness. As you focus, imaginary images of faces intermingle with the shapes, forcing you to accept their meaning. You shudder, remembering the scenario etched out on the plaster. Light suddenly illuminates the window from outside, hastening you towards it. Peeping through the half-open heavy drapes, your eyes survey a tableau you never imagined you would witness again. The figures standing in a circle include you, a younger you, a different you. In the middle of the circle, a young naked woman is spread-eagled on a rough wooden bench. You observe yourself stepping forwards, mouthing words. Although no sounds reach the window, you know exactly what the incantation is. The other you raises a long bone knife and your eyes join together as the blade plunges into the sacrificial chest. You faint.

You wake in your room, a fine covering of perspiration coating your body. As you sit up, fear envelopes you as you realise your hands are covered in blood.

Trust

Phil Horscroft

Jake stood deep in the shop doorway watching the men through the carefully orchestrated clutter of the window display.

They were sitting at two tables pushed together on the edge of the food court, obviously expecting more company; sharing jokes and showing photographs of grandchildren, bikes and boats. They were a mixed bunch, four men, one relatively small, two big and one huge; two neat and clean in chinos, pressed polo tops and polished shoes, one in a suit and one in old jeans, a T-shirt and work boots, but something about them whispered 'old soldiers'.

They looked to be in their early sixties, but still with an air of confidence, erect and capable; even dangerous, if you were impressionable and watched a lot of films. Despite their age an observant watcher would have seen shoulders still square and muscular, bellies that looked big but weren't drooping over their belts and still with a flat front; relaxed muscle mass, or well exercised visceral fat.

It had been a difficult stalk, but Jake had gotten within thirty yards of the group without being noticed and was feeling pleased with himself. It was what he did for a living after all, but this had been an opportunity to practise this special slice of the dark arts without the usual stress or fear and he was enjoying himself. He waited patiently for a group of young men to amble past the doorway towards his target, laughing and talking loudly, and he moved out behind them to try and cover the last stretch in their wake, not really expecting to succeed, he knew his targets too well.

As he walked he watched the men at the table. Skip,

their former team leader, was sitting quietly, smiling and letting the banter flow around him. "Keeping my powder dry," he used to say. "Trying to keep up and failing," they would laughingly retort. Big Ugly was there, throwing his not inconsiderable bulk around as usual, leaning over Ferret and prodding him in the side as he embellished another never-ending story. Ferret, as always, betrayed no emotion. He sat straight and still, despite the muscular weight of his friend; his head turning like a laid back, hungry owl, his eyes constantly moving; settling on nothing, noticing everything; searching, probing for lost threats.

Little Ugly sat, as always, across the table from Big Ugly, chatting to Skip and showing him photos, probably of the wife he adored and their uncountable brood of raucous, much-loved children. Or his boat. Close call. Although the two Uglys were close friends, Little Ugly was the only one in the team who wouldn't tolerate the big guy's unconscious intimidations, and he always kept his distance, which Big Ugly never noticed.

Jake was halfway to the table when Ferret found him behind the group of young men and nodded twice in his direction. Big Ugly broke off his storytelling and looked in the direction Ferret was indicating, his face lighting up with a wide smile.

"Hey Jake! Sneaking up as usual. How ya doin' feller?"

Jake walked the last few yards to the table while his old comrades called their welcomes. Everyone was smiling and, apparently happy to see him, and none of them were surprised at his surreptitious approach. Anything else would have unsettled them

"You're on your meds then, Ferret?" Jake called. "Ten yards close before you saw me there. Not as if we're in the jungle."

"Fifteen, and we are in the jungle, just fewer bushes."

"How you doing, my friend" Jake asked Ferret while shaking Skip's hand.

"Yeah I'm doing OK."

Ferret was the best lookout man in the business, primarily because he was the paranoid survivor of growing up the only black kid in a Dr Barnados home in the sixties. Back in the day they had been one of the best close observation teams in 39 Brigade, Northern Ireland, and had spent years tasked to 14th Intelligence Company and various other shadowy organisations. Not always watching, sometimes doing some truly outrageous things and surviving, much to their own and everyone else's surprise.

Although Jake had suggested this get-together, he was a little sad they'd all showed up. He had hoped one or two might cry off but known they never would. They'd been through too much together and they all genuinely liked each other. They always turned up and Jake knew this could be the last time, but he had a job to do and duty, as ever, came first, particularly as his current boss was fully aware of the situation. They would understand, eventually. One of the team had broken the code and was making a mess, and rule one of mess-making, you clean up your own. Preferably before the neighbours start pretending they can't smell anything.

"How you doing, Jake? Surprised you got a day off with all this shit going on."

Skip was the only one of the group who knew for certain Jake was still in the game. He assumed Jake was a watcher, or Mobile Surveillance Officer, with the Security Service, he'd been interviewed as part of Jake's positive vetting, but he was unaware that Jake was currently attached to the Met as a liaison officer.

"I'm important nowadays, Skip. I say to this man, go, and he goeth," Jake smiled.

He thought he detected a spark of inquiry behind Skip's eyes. Did Skip know or suspect? Jake couldn't see how but you never really knew for certain. You just had to press on along the tightrope regardless and let the terror-daemons trash their room in the back of your mind, until you had space and time to whip and cajole them back into order.

"You can pay the bill then, seeing as how you're doing so well."

"I thought you were rich, Skip? Didn't you inherit a couple of scrapyards?" Big Ugly called.

"Speaking of family, how's Poppy?" Little Ugly asked.

"Yeah, she's well thanks. She's coming over later. Say hi and scam some dosh out of her uncles," Skip smiled

"What's she doing now?" Ferret asked.

"She's working for me in the yard. Runs the office."

"She'll need the money then," Ferret said with his usual deadpan delivery.

"You sure it's not you working for her?" Big Ugly teased.

"Poppy still with the dickhead?" Ferret asked with his usual tact and diplomacy.

"As it happens, no, she finally managed to pull the trigger and dumped him yesterday. I sacked his arse as soon as she told me," Skip laughed.

The whole group cheered. Poppy was their first and spoilt favourite, and her latest choice of boyfriend had rung everybody's alarm bells from day one. Everybody but Poppy who, they thought, had been infatuated with 'the dickhead' as they all habitually referred to him; preferably when he was there in the room. All muscle and no 'bottom' had been the unanimous consensus.

Driving into the car park of the small shopping centre where the old sweats were toasting his calamities in Earl Grey and

Americano, Dickhead was truly, deeply, *off the cliff-edge mad.*

That bitch had dumped him! Him!

He'd had plans, big plans; and the bitch had blown them all out of the water with her betrayal. Poppy was Skip's only family and he'd taken it for granted he would eventually inherit the yards. Now, in a flicker of mascara, his dreams were ironic barbs in his head. His mum had just said, "How will you pay me housekeeping if you've lost your job?" and his 'mates' had all laughed when he told them in the pub. The iceberg collision of the break up and scorn and indifference of his family and friends were stoking his anger beyond his limited control and he was full steam ahead for the bottom of the pond. The frenzied determination to see his tormentors pay was made almost bearable by the poetic justice that they would be the ones to make it possible.

He'd worked for Skip in the scrapyard while going out with that bitch, Poppy, and he'd kept his eyes open, seeing things he definitely wasn't meant to see. It had been easy to sneak into the yard once Skip was gone. The dogs hadn't got the memo saying he was sacked and he'd had his own keys cut months ago. He'd gone straight to the old car behind the portakabin office and forced open the boot, helping himself to one of the handguns stored in there. The ammunition had been right there next to the guns and he'd snatched up a full magazine, slamming it into the gun with a satisfying click. Holding the gun made him feel surprisingly good; strong and getting his control back; control was everything. He'd jumped into his car with a grin on his face that would have had Bruce out of his slippers and looking for his cape before the bat signal was even warm.

Dickhead screeched to a stop outside the entrance to the shopping centre and scooped up the gun from the passenger footwell where it had fallen off the seat. The thought of a parking ticket worried him but he wouldn't be in there very long and didn't want to waste time running around the car park afterwards. Poppy was always laughing at his inability to remember where he'd left the car. He stalked through the doors of the centre shoving the gun into the pocket of his hoodie. The bitch was meeting her dad in there that afternoon and as he walked he started to worry about getting close enough. If he had to run around trying to catch her that would just be a massive show-up. His rage had driven him this far but now his fear decided it might be a good idea to consult his animal cunning and he stopped to try and work out a plan. He stood in an alcove of the mall for a few minutes, drawing a blank, until a young girl walked past him pushing a sleeping baby in a buggy. Noticing he was standing by the entrance to the toilets, something masquerading as inspiration struck. He followed the young girl into the ladies.

The madness acid was eating his reason away one brain cell at a time and the tattered remnants of his mind were having fun making outrageous suggestions; just to see how far he could be pushed? Right at that moment one of the imps was telling him that having a kid in a buggy would give him some cover and he could hide the gun in a fold of the buggy's hood, where it would be easier to get at than in his pocket. It would also show his mates, and that bitch, Poppy, just how tough he could be. He needed to get close. Not just to make certain he didn't miss, but also because he wanted to enjoy the terror on their faces before he showed them the cost of disrespect.

The young girl turned to look at him with a mildly amused expression, which quickly turned to horrified disbelief as he took the gun out of his pocket and pointed it at her face.

"Gimme the kid, bitch!"

The girl opened her mouth to scream and he pulled the trigger.

The gun gave a loud click and nothing at all came out of the barrel. They both stopped and looked at the gun in confusion and disbelief. He was looking at the gun and shaking it, trying to figure out what was wrong, when the young girl recovered her wits first and hit him on the end of his nose with her bag.

He shat himself a little and staggered back against the door, his eyes streaming tears and his nose other things. "What did she have in that bag?" The girl, fighting frantically for her child, tried to follow up and knee him in the balls but he instinctively flinched and she missed and hit his thigh. He was ducking his head and flailing his arms, trying not to get hit in the face again, and the girl was bulling into him, giving him no space, desperately trying to stop the nightmare. Her luck ran out when Dickhead's thrashing around with the gun accidently hit her hard in the eye, shocking her out of fight mode. He looked up when he felt the gun hit something and saw the girl reeling away from him, hands to her face. Finding what he thought of as his courage he stepped forward and hit her hard on the head with the gun. The girl gave a strangled sob and fell against the wall. He giggled and hit her on the head some more, partly to be certain but mostly because he was enjoying it.

Once he was sure the girl was no longer a threat he looked at the bloodied gun. Had he forgotten to cock the damn thing? He pulled back the slide and pushed it forward hard. He wondered if that was right and thought about trying it out. The madness was pommeling him on like a bulldozer and he looked down at the kid in the buggy.

The thought scared and excited him as he pointed the gun down at the sleeping child. He was squeezing the trigger when the thought of how much noise the gun might make stopped him. He had no idea how loud it would be but did remember Skip saying they made quite a bang when telling one of his rare war stories. Attracting attention might mean a delay, and if he made a mess of the kid he might not be able to use it as cover. He looked at the girl but that would surely be just as loud? While the tattered flag of his mind was twitching back and forth in the gusts of indecision the thought of a parking ticket spiked in his head again. He decided he would just have to take a chance on the gun and get on with the plan. The baby had, amazingly, slept through the entire episode and he grabbed the buggy, looked down at the girl, bleeding and unmoving on the floor, giggled some more and hurriedly backed out of the toilets to go and look for his next victim. *He could get used to this.*

Ferret spotted Dickhead coming thirty yards away and an old alarm came blinking out of a far and forgotten box at the back of his mind.

Something wasn't right.

The body language was all wrong: **twenty-five yards.**

The dickhead was pushing somebody's baby in a buggy but he was walking like he was heading for a fight: **twenty yards.**

His shoulders were hunched and his face was twitching: **fifteen yards.**

Most worryingly, his hand was hidden in the fold of the buggy's hood: **twelve yards.**

The warning signs were piling up and all of Ferret's instincts were prodding him out of his urbanity: **nine yards.**

The decider was the blood smeared on Dickhead's hooded sweater and dripping from his nose: **seven yards.**

Ferret cursed his slowness and remembered a phrase

from his training almost too late. "Wrong and embarrassed is preferable to right and beaten."

"ENEMY LEFT!" Ferret said loudly and, picking up a cup, pushed his chair away from his legs as he stood up. The others all stopped talking and turned to look at whatever had caught Ferret's attention. Jake grabbed a plate and a cup as he got up, cursing his old bones for slowing him down.

Dickhead was too busy looking for Poppy and wondering if his nose was broken and why his arse felt damp and sore to pay much attention to what his target was doing. He was ten feet away before realising the five old men were all staring at him and getting up from their chairs. This wasn't in the script! He grabbed for the gun and raised it towards the men, who were all now moving in different directions.

"GUN!" Big Ugly shouted and threw his plate at Dickhead's face before rolling to the ground to clear the others field of fire. The plate was immediately joined by an astonishing fusillade of tableware from the others. He hunched his shoulders and ducked his head, the cascade of crockery making him close his eyes in fear. He held the gun out like a shield and jerked the trigger.

It was at that precise moment that everybody, except Dickhead, realised he'd stolen the right gun but the wrong ammunition. When picking up the gun he had read .357 on the box but in his rush and stupidity had picked up a magazine out of a case of .375; just enough difference to make a difference, and when he had pushed the slide forward he'd forced the round into the chamber ensuring an unhappy ending. The barrel exploded and the dickhead squealed in agony as a piece of his finger was blown off, landing next to a spoon on the screaming baby's lap. Small hot fragments of the bullet and barrel flew in all directions.

A piece hit Ferret on the arm as he punched Dickhead in the neck. Another fragment scored a groove in Jake's forearm as he kicked Dickhead on the knee and grabbed his hair to force him down onto the floor where Little Ugly jumped, knees first, onto his back, pinning him down. The dickhead stopped worrying about parking tickets and began a detailed examination of a floor tile.

"Bloody hell! What happened there?" Little Ugly gasped.

"Where'd he get a gun?" Big Ugly asked as he got up off the floor 'accidentally' treading heavily on the weeping Dickhead's injured hand, breaking two of his remaining fingers.

"I think that's a question my guv'nors will soon be asking you, Skip" Jake said.

"Not sure what you mean there, Jake?"

"Poppy's had an epiphany and she's on her way to Spain with her new boyfriend; and probably most of your money," Jake told his oldest friend and newest arrest.

Corona La Famiglia

Gini Scanlan

Stephen

I knew that it was bad before he spoke;
ischemic stroke. Their faces said it all.
Saliva drained so that you didn't choke;
I tried to read the doctor's hurried scrawl.
The MRI had shown the site of clots
that blocked the flow of blood around your brain,
the damaged places showing up as spots.
They said you might not walk or speak again.
But you were so determined not to be
disabled or a burden, so you had
to rehabilitate to the degree
that you could be a husband and a dad.
Four years have passed and I can never say
how close you came to dying on that day.

Amber

How close you came to dying on that day
you crashed your car; it troubles me still now;
and that the man who hit you got away
with just a tiny scratch upon his brow.
You are my rock, the oldest of my girls;
forthright, outspoken, honest to a fault,
with rosebud lips and shining chestnut curls,
our reigning Queen of the verbal assault.
Yet quietly determined to succeed
in every undertaking you create,
with merciless ambition guaranteed,
a woman who's in charge of her own fate.
Your talent shining, singing pure and loud
a daughter who will always make me proud.

Elicia

A daughter who will always make me proud,
my second girl and BA Undergrad;
eccentric ways, creativeness allowed,
untidiness that almost drives me mad.
With Barbie figure, Marilyn élan,
eclectic style so that you look the part;
Bohemian. You have a lifetime plan
to mend all broken cognizance with art.
The broken wrists that threatened your career
long healed, but leave you constantly in pain.
But these twelve months have been a better year,
you've taken back control of your domain.
I see your work on show and am beguiled,
it makes me think of when you were a child.

Celeste

It makes me think of when you were a child
when we go back to lush Northumberland;
us living on the farm, you running wild,
Dad tending livestock with the hired hand.
The simple life had suited you so well;
days feeding hens and fishing in the pool,
or walking in the woods and on the fell,
imaginary games, and your first school.
As I look at you now I see that girl,
untroubled *joie de vivre* and sense of fun;
and wonder how you'll change as you unfurl
into a young woman; my youngest one.
Never without a graze upon your shin,
I love your scruffy curls and cheeky grin.

Zachary

I love your scruffy curls and cheeky grin,
your wayward hair a gentle honeyed hue,
a hint of wispy hair upon your chin,
with rosy cheeks and eyes of piercing blue.
You had a child whilst still a boy yourself,
you took it in your stride and will again.
To see you now no one could ever tell
what a wilful youth you were back then.
You turned your life around, became a man,
you've toed the line and hold a steady job,
and love your little son; eagerly plan
to marry soon. Our first child wed; I'll sob.
And so will dad although he's a tough guy;
you are the apple of your father's eye.

Lewis

You are the apple of your father's eye,
though who you favour most, I can't decide.
I knew when I first saw you I would cry,
reminding me of my baby that died.
A stranger welcomed into our mad clan,
our grandson, such a happy little lad,
a funny, bright and handsome tiny man
and when you smile you look just like your dad.
Your parents do send videos to me
by email, still it cuts me like a knife
you live so far away. I barely see
you so I miss the milestones of your life.
But memories of you I can't erase;
your perfect tiny toes and flawless face.

Grace

Your perfect tiny toes and flawless face
are my abiding memory of you.
I never will forget our one embrace
when all our hopes and dreams had fallen through.
All the signs were there that I could think;
the pregnancy confirmed, I felt fulfilled.
The scan said 'baby girl'; I painted pink
and emptied all the shops of lace and frills.
You were a gift from God; we'd tried so long
to have a child so when you were conceived
I was complete. But then it went so wrong,
and eight months later I was left bereaved.
Your dad was so distraught when I awoke,
I knew that it was bad before he spoke.

100 Worder: Shades of Life

Peter Sandling

My first memories were of colours. Kaleidoscopes of hues surrounding people like an angel's halo. Each combination of shades signifying the emotions and true hidden thoughts of those around me. White for peace with flecks of pink showing love and compassion, to dark grey containing shards of black for evil. An artist's palette of bewilderment.

My life has been regulated by these observations. Always moulded by warnings or confirmations of intent. Relationships have been impossible when each life unfolds before me. Loneliness has become inevitable. I shudder to imagine the future. What other fearful gifts will evolution perpetrate on me?

The Night Train

Margaret Potter

Sleeping on duty was a sackable offence.

Eric had been caught napping before, but working alone in the signal box on the lonely stretch of line sometimes proved a challenge. Nine times out of ten he kept the lonely vigil without any hiccups. It was not a popular posting but Eric, a bit of a loner, relished in the quiet and uninterrupted life. Not for him the busy stations further up the line. The deep railway cutting in the heart of the moors suited him perfectly. Once, when a hiker became lost, she had stumbled upon Eric's signal box. Eric had shone his torch and lit up the startled hiker's face demanding, "Who goes there?"

The hiker had put up an arm to shield her eyes and with wavering voice shouted back. "It's Jill, Jill from London. I'm lost."

Eric had wearily climbed down the wooden steps from the box to the track. The hiker, clearly pleased to find another human after wandering endlessly on the moors, made to cross.

"Stop! Wait!" shouted Eric.

He examined his watch and, satisfied that the express which roared through the cutting wasn't due for another ten minutes, beckoned the girl over.

"Come on. Cross quickly."

Once inside the signal box, the hiker warmed herself by the stove. She explained she was staying at the inn in the village for a short walking holiday. She had become disorientated and had been wandering around for what seemed like hours.

"Oh, that be the haunted inn," said Eric. "It's only a few hundred yards from here."

"Haunted?"

Eric laughed. He hadn't had so much fun in ages.

"Well, thems that stay there have reported sightings."

The hiker, apparently heartened by the warmth of the signal box, seemed eager to hear more but Eric, on hearing the bell ring in the box, tended to his work.

The hiker watched as the signalman returned a sort of Morse code on the bell, then proceeded to pull the heavy signal handles forward. Within minutes, the eleven twenty from the north approached in the cutting, its sheer power shaking the signal box and rattling the tea cups, plates and glasses.

Jill covered her ears as the roar of the express tore past. Eric, used to such happenings, could see that his new acquaintance was visibly shaken. He grinned.

"That be the lion. I call it that, the eleven twenty express 'cause it roars past, same time every night."

The hiker suddenly looked very weary.

Eric offered her a cup of tea, bringing out an old battered biscuit tin from the cupboard. Jill shook her head. "Many thanks but haunted or not, I must return to the inn.

I have supper waiting and I'm in need of a hot bath and sleep."

Eric told her where to find the inn.

"It's very close to this deep railway cutting. Just up on the top of here and turn right. You can't miss it."

The proprietor of the inn had been worried. It seemed he didn't get many customers out of season and was worried when Jill had been gone for hours.

"Thank goodness," he said when she finally pushed open the door.

Jill sighed; the inn's lights had been such a welcoming sight shining brightly on the hillside. With the door firmly shut and a small glass of wine in hand, she asked the proprietor about any ghosts at the inn. She explained she had been told by the signalman at the cutting.

"He was most accommodating but the express train, the eleven twenty, why it roared through there and frightened me half to death."

The proprietor's face turned white, his hands trembling. He busied himself behind the bar, stacking glasses, tidying bottles, avoiding the hiker's gaze.

Jill went on to tell him about the cosiness of the signal box with its warm stove, deep old armchairs and book-lined shelves.

The proprietor poured out two drinks. He drank the whisky himself and with trembling hands, offered the glass of wine to Jill.

"That signal box has been empty for years. No trains pass through there nowadays, ever since…"

He stopped, as if frightened to elaborate.

"Since?"

"…the old signalman, Eric I think he was called, was killed by the eleven twenty over twenty years ago. Apparently he was asleep on duty and awoke just a few minutes before it was due. It's said he was woken by a shout and stumbled down to the track to stop a hiker from crossing the line to his signal box. The hiker was saved but Eric was killed instantly…"

Brain Contradictions

Amber Graelin

From 1961 to 2010, your marvellous mind jumps about in
an array of fact and fiction.
Lies and truth fall from your tongue and entertain our
inquisitive minds,
even now.
You're here and you're gone and we're here
treasuring
you.
Every word we
hang
onto.
Your eyes brighten and dull and flicker from confusion to
recognition.
Your memories and stories leave us with
more questions
than you could answer now.
Germany or London; we travel as you tell what's on your
mind in that moment.
We laugh and dance as you sporadically sing.
We secretly cry in the night's darkness;
alone but together.
Your former greatness is there but missing.
Our tears are grateful but our hearts;
broken.

**Dedication: This poem is dedicated to my dad, my
father-in-law and to everyone living with any sort of
brain-altering condition. Keep smiling, stay strong and
never stop loving.**

Black Swan/White Swan

Paul Westgate

My head was full of memories. Each one, the moment it appeared, bringing forth more. Each one of those more in turn, and tears fell. Olga was dead. It shouldn't really have been a shock; she was a good fifteen years older than me. I suppose it was that I thought of her as always being there, somewhere.

The young woman on the telephone had been matter-of-fact, detached, merely wanting an interview because Olga had died and I had known her. I was surprised. She must have dug pretty deeply to find the connection to me.

It was my aunt who got me into the company. I think she was a sponsor or something. I don't believe that Madame – we had to call her Madame – had been too pleased to have me. But after a month or so she must have thought I was good enough – box office receipts aren't lightly put at risk – and she started putting me into productions. I was the youngest and the most recent to join the company, by a good few years in both cases. Even after a year I was still the newcomer. I wasn't liked.

I remember when we heard that the company was to have a season with Olga Tourischeva. I was excited and went on and on about it until Eleanor, in that languid voice she liked to affect, told me to shut up. "Oh do put a sock it in, darling," she'd said. They all thought they were oh so sophisticated, so tried hard not to show any excitement at all. But that was all just bluff. In the early 1930s, Olga Tourischeva had been a leading light in modern dance for at least a decade, her influence spreading far beyond her own dance company. They knew as well as I that we were incredibly fortunate to have a season with her.

The season was to consist of three dances choreographed by Olga and featuring her in the principal roles. Each would run for six performances. The tickets had sold out within a few days of the box office opening. Olga appeared at the theatre at 7.30 on a Monday morning. From that day she worked the entire company – dancers, musicians, lighting, wardrobe, even front of house – hard. When Sylvia's Achilles tendon went with the sound of a pistol shot, Olga barely paused.

The company was all female. Modern dance was almost exclusively a female dance form in those days. I'd seen a lot of good-looking female bodies either skimpily dressed or completely naked but Olga's body was simply wonderful. It wasn't that she was beautiful as such or even that her legs or breasts or bottom were particularly stunning. It was that her whole body, the way it moved, the way she carried it, was the most expressive I have ever seen. I used to sit and watch her just walk across a room or raise a cup to her lips, just for the pleasure of seeing her move.

After two full weeks with only Sunday as a rest day, Olga sent us home for a day while she and Madame agreed the final details and casting for the three pieces. When we returned, Madame announced who would dance what role or roles. It was like being picked for a team at school, wondering when or if your name was going to be called or whether you'd end up last and having the teacher put you in a team. There was no discussion and any overt display of emotion, elation or despair, was considered, as Eleanor said, 'Frightfully bad form darling'.

I was both elated and in despair. I had been selected for only one piece but it was the best, the season's finale – Black Swan/White Swan – and I was to dance the part of the white swan, which was second principal. But, and this was the cruellest blow, I was to understudy Muriel. This

110

meant, barring something happening to Muriel, that I would sit out every performance. I had no other role in the season. When, three days before the first performance, Muriel fell ill with food poisoning, suspicion fell on me. Proof, if any were needed, was that I had taken Olga and Muriel a cup of tea after the previous day's rehearsal. The rest of the company promptly sent me to Coventry. It was only when Muriel telephoned to say that her sister had come down with the same thing and that she thought it was some grilled chicken they'd both had the night before, that they relented. But I was not forgiven for taking Muriel's place. She was popular, I was not.

I doubt that Black Swan/White Swan has been performed anywhere in the last thirty years. That is modern dance – it needs to be... well, it needs to continue to innovate, to challenge, so there's no place for yesterday's dances. The story is straightforward, simple almost, but it is exquisitely beautiful. The white swan is young and innocent and is gradually entranced and ultimately seduced by the older and more experienced black swan. Its beauty comes from the gradual expression of each swan's different emotions, which become one and the same in the very final steps.

I will never forget that performance. Our bodies seemed to be made for this dance. Moving around and across each other, our hands touching and stroking, the other dancers sliding between, temporarily separating us until we found a way to elude them and come together once again. In the final few movements of the dance I took a risk. In the kiss before the final movement, I opened my mouth slightly and let my tongue delicately slide across Olga's lips. In that moment, when the music seemed to hang endlessly on a single note, Olga's lips parted and her tongue gently caressed mine. I didn't need to simulate the shuddering ecstasy that is the climax of the dance. Held in position by Olga, I was oblivious until the thunderous applause brought me out of it. We shared five encores that night.

The following day Muriel returned to the theatre and declared herself fit and well. After a further rehearsal Olga agreed and I watched the remaining performances from the wings.

Walking, sometimes dancing through my memories had taken up most of the morning. I would have to be getting ready for the journalist when she arrived. I wondered what I should say to her. What would she want to know? I wouldn't talk of the moment Olga and I had shared at the end of the dance. I have kept it safe in my heart all this time. I would simply talk of how I had once known the great Olga Tourischeva and had danced the White Swan to her Black Swan.

The Black Glove

Julie Kendall

In the glove compartment I look and see
One black glove that don't belong to me
I wonder who has been in here today.
Was she blonde, brunette or grey?

I see you turn red, I feel so hurt
Did she have a very short skirt?
Legs that went right up her bum
Guess you had your share of fun.

Did you take her to that park?
What did you do? Bet it was dark
You sit there so calm and quiet?
Please deny it, I hoped you might.

He stops the car, door opens for me
Something falls, what could that be?
Oh dear I cringe I'm sorry my love
As out of my pocket, falls a glove.

You are suspicious, my love is true
The glove's in there waiting for you
Now trust me please from now on
For like your gloves we two belong.

Forsaken Love

Peter Sandling

She was my first love.

I had no point of reference, just weird feelings in various parts of my body that instinctively forced me to accept something was different.

What was it about her?

It was obvious. The short blonde hair, those long legs framed by her mini skirt, full lips and those blue eyes that I could stare at for hours. We held hands walking home from school, planned cinema dates, picnics by the lido and eventually tea at her house. Naturally, her parents didn't like me. Not many people did – something about the way I looked. I knew the comments.

"Really Lucy, what are you doing with him? I hear he's a thug. You could do so much better."

"You don't know him like I do, Daddy. He's not like people say."

The problem was that I was like people said: a nasty bit of work, someone to avoid, a social misfit. That didn't mean that I had no feelings, especially for Lucy. I would do anything for her. I was consciously different when we were together. I became caring and thoughtful. Why couldn't I be like that at other times with other people?

When I left school, Lucy stayed on to do A-levels and talked about university. I got a job labouring on a building site. She said she loved me and we could marry when she graduated. I suggested living together at my house straight away. Her father was not pleased. She started broadening her social group. Intense young people who saw the world in a wider context.

She would say, "Duncan said this and Margie said that."

I was forced to spend time in their company and hated it. I felt inferior, even though they tried to be friendly and inclusive towards me, I still felt patronised and became petulant.

Our first row was instigated over a comment that Martin, one of the older members of the group, said about a trip to an art show, wondering if it was my cup of tea.

"Do you think I'm a moron; that I can't appreciate art?" I said, my anger clearly visible.

Later, Lucy said, "Why did you react like that? Martin didn't mean anything by it."

"Didn't he? You know he fancies you. Can't wait to be with you, trying to get into your knickers."

"I don't want to talk about that sort of thing. I don't fancy him. It's you I love."

My position in the group exposed all my insecurities. I knew I was only tolerated because of Lucy. It started to eat away at our relationship.

The following day, Lucy was leaving to visit her aunt in Leeds with her family. She came round before departing.

"I think we need to have a talk when I get back."

"You mean about last night?"

"Yes, and other things." She kissed me. "See you Friday."

I thought her eyes looked sad.

I didn't see her Friday. Her father told me she had a stomach upset. I phoned repeatedly over the weekend, always being told she was unavailable. I suspected she'd told her parents everything and they'd continued their relentless campaign to separate us. Monday evening I'd planned to go to her

115

house on my way home from work. I was invited in by her father.

"Lucy's not here. She's away until the end of the week."

"Making sure she stays away from me, is that it?"

He ignored my comments.

"Do you love my daughter?" he asked.

I was a little thrown by such a direct question.

"Of course I do, I always have."

"Then stop seeing her and let her get on with her life."

"I want to be in her life."

"You'll eventually ruin it for her."

"No I won't."

He looked me up and down. "Look at you. No prospects, no education, you react violently to anything not to your liking. Do you think that's what an intelligent, forward thinking young woman wants? Do you?"

"But I love her."

"Then let her go," he said angrily. "If she marries you she'll be pregnant within a year, stuck in some council flat and any hopes and dreams she could have fulfilled will be over forever. You'd deny her a career and she'd end up with a life revolving around the pub and football."

I felt like punching him as hard as I could. I knew it was what he wanted. The display of what he thought I was really like. One final act to destroy our relationship. I stormed off. I went to the pub to get excessively drunk, trying to pick a fight to expel all my anger and humiliation. When I squared up to a man at the bar, he pushed me and I fell over unable to get up.

The next morning I was hungover and felt sick. Despite that, the events of the previous few months, especially the night before, started to stalk my mind. I looked around. I occupied most of the upstairs of my father's house and realised it was a pig sty. The small kitchen had unwashed dishes in the sink, the waste bin was overflowing, and there was dirty washing piled in the corner. Lucy's house was immaculate, a standard she was used to and expected. She had friends who drove flash cars, talked about holidays in France and the Greek islands. A normal, acceptable way of life for them all.

"Lucy, you must come down to our parents' house in Biarritz. Why not bring George with you?" as if I was an afterthought. I started to think about everything. Perhaps her dad was right. I was a loser who'd stop her from ever achieving anything important. That made me feel even more depressed. It took several days and troubled nights to admit to myself that I had to break up with her. I agonisingly wrote her a letter, dropping it off at her house to be forwarded. I knew I had to be brutal. I told her I didn't love her anymore and lied about seeing somebody else. I wanted her to hate me, forget me, not come round trying to get back together because I knew ultimately I couldn't resist her.

She wrote back saying she loved me, her life would be over without me, was there any chance of me changing my mind?

I didn't write back.

Eventually, she went to university in Scotland and I never saw her again.

Over the years, I married and divorced twice, had numerous liaisons, no children and rented my father's house from the council when he died. I often thought about Lucy and what her life was like.

My second wife, Mavis, was obsessed with social media. Her affair started there. She'd put me on Facebook. It seemed pointless but I'd agreed. She'd sorted out several profile pictures for my page, none of which I liked. I eventually chose a photograph of a pint of Guinness. I was glad that she was not pleased. I eventually blocked all information but for some reason kept it live.

Lucy must have contacted every George Hoggs because one day I had a request.

"Are you the George Hoggs who was at Cross Keys Comprehensive in Harringay between 1965 and 1970?"

It was her! I stared at her picture. How good she looked. It seemed her whole life was on display. Album photos of a family life on beaches, skiing holidays, graduations and grandchildren. Suddenly the tall man in the online scrapbook disappeared from the pages.

"Yes," I hastily replied. "It was me."

She suggested afternoon tea at the Fenwick hotel in the centre of town. I would explain about the letter. Did she ever believe it? Would there still be a spark of love for me? Mine for her was never extinguished.

I arrived early, sitting at the bar, observing the flow of people. She arrived on time in a jaguar SUV. I recognised the driver, her son. He gave her a quick kiss and drove off. As she entered she looked stunning. Tall, slim, lightly tanned, her high heels accentuating her long legs. My mind filled with evidence of her life, totally the opposite of mine. Several of the lobby pillars had mirrors on them and I took in my reflection. I'd gained weight recently, my only suit jacket tight, the trousers supported by braces. I'd shaved earlier but it didn't look like it. I felt sick staring at this stranger. I had nothing to offer her when I was young and realised I had nothing to offer her now, only love and that would never be enough. She had her back to me. I walked towards her, pausing, smelling her perfume, looking down on that long neck she loved me to kiss. I could have reached out, touched her on the shoulder, said so many things but I just continued walking through the double doors.

MahaKali

Bianca Eleanor

The vast cosmic black womb,
Kali the divine creator,
barefoot pounding Soil, sparks fly,
jewel colour flames embrace you, as you command
destructions dance.
Mother of flame
Rider of tigers
Shyama
Naked, truth and freedom.
Blood drenched tongue hangs south,
crows and cries of savage tribes,
beastly growls of bodiless beings.
Your Voice is heard through screaming labour pains,
and the thrashing of drums on battlefields.
Your palm extended, S T I L L; you stand, in the midst of terror,
Violence hath never been so loving.
Presence seen in tsunamis that wash away structure,
bitter ice hailstorms that transform landscapes,
heavens flaming rocks, scorching through forests.
Fierce is your love, like unbridled passion without reason.
Your energy is the essence of liberation;
felt in the moment a rebel impales a fallen dictator.
Shattering limits, invoking 'the serpents wisdom' to
writhe through our veins.
Warrior spirit, birthed by ego slain.
Our poisons brewed into nectar, that enriches our souls.
Kali Maa
Ecstasy, infinite,
let us taste the freedom of your wild dance,
to know your love is to feel allure in the depths of grief,

unite our authentic being in consciousness, under the stars.
Surrender to time, the all destroyer,
until we receive your kiss and lay around your neck,
transcendent unto the light of your darkness.
Om Aim Hreem Kleem Chamundaye Yai Viche Swaha.

Observations of the Reaper

Dave Traer

You sit on that same jetty, facing outwards towards the river's open mouth.

The sun is setting, casting thin red lines over the receding tide. Gulls scavenge deep into the cold, wet mud for morsels of black nourishment. Every day you sit on those weathered planks. Every day you wait. From daybreak till dusk you wait. From twilight to the darkness before the dawn you wait. *He will come, he must come, he promised.*

So you wait.

The chilled easterly wind cuts into your wraithlike limbs. A scarf covers your nose and mouth, but not your eyes, not your ears. They must stay open and alert, even though you see and hear nothing. *Tonight he will come, tonight he must come, he promised.*

It starts to rain, not hard rain, not irritating drizzle that saturates. Not like yesterday; that deluge of wetness will never dry out. Deep pools of water left in its wake will never evaporate.

You turn into the waves of rising mist and you wait. The air feels different tonight, more intense. *Yes, tonight it feels right, tonight he will come.*

You remember your first visit to that place. You remember that night, that hot summer night. He was there on the island. He promised that wherever you were, he would find you. You believed him then. He compelled you to believe him. You remember the place, Hole Haven Creek. You remember that isolated, stone sentinel, proudly standing by the grey waters. The Kynoch Hotel filled with palatial

122

grandeur, where time itself seemed vanquished beneath its faceless clock tower. You remember staring across the water, thankful that you stood a safe distance from the distant explosive works upriver. You remember the factory's owners, whom you came there to meet. With the increasing likelihood of a European war, you were seeking a profitable investment opportunity. You dined with your newfound friends and joined in their merriment. They persuaded you to make up the number in the gathering of the thirteen. *He was there. You saw him. You heard him call your name. He will return. He will return tonight. He must. He promised.*

That's when life got better. Much better. Wild, outrageous parties. You could hear him laughing. You could hear him singing. The melody still haunts your memory, it resounds deep within your skull. Yesterday you felt it again. Yesterday you remembered the words. Yesterday that same haunting tune travelled on the wind, pulsated with the pounding rain. *He is close. Yes, tonight he will come, tonight he must come.*

Far into the distance a fog horn vibrates the air. You shudder as waves of sound brush past. You turn into the mist. Perhaps it is him. Perhaps, tonight, your patience will, at last, be rewarded. *Yes, he will come, he must.* The rain gets harder. It batters your hood, it pounds your dark cloak. You sit and you wait. You sit and you remember.

You remember his voice, deep within your corrupted mind, compelling you to return to that place. You remember the uncomfortable coach journey from the capital. You remember the absinth, that green liquid which addled your crazed minds. You recall the amusement as you and your reckless companions, slipped and splashed

123

over the stepping stones. You were far older and yet you appeared much younger than the rest. They thought you had far fewer years behind you. It made you feel good. It made you feel alive.

You remember laughing as the horses struggled to drag their burden across the deepening creek. You thought you saw him sitting beside the driver. He was grinning insanely. Was he the cause for the horses' unrest, or was it just a trick of the light? You shivered, hoping it was the latter.

The rain becomes hail. You perceive the music. Yes, it returns. It returns with the wind-driven icy pellets. Its melody drags you back to that place. Back to that night. You hear the laughing. You see the women. Oh yes, the women. He stands in the doorway and he watches. He laughs, he sings.

He must come, the memories have never been so vivid. *Yes, tonight he will come.*

You are privileged, you have royal blood. You are, like the clock tower, untouched by time. Your perpetual youth and wealth can never be questioned. Those who dig and delve will suffer and suffer badly. It is your Hellfire club. Not theirs. Only yours. The others are mere scavengers. Uncouth lowlifes with no social standing. Not like you, a man of substance. A man of substantial means. Yet, despite their lack of breeding, they are fun. Where are they now? They are probably still there. Still laughing, still singing, still drinking that unforgiving liquor. You should go back and join them. Why do you still sit and wait? Why do you waste your time waiting on that cold wet pier? Surely, when he does return, he will go to that hotel. That is where he looked happy. That is where he laughed. That is where he sang. He won't be as joyous out there in the cold and damp. Leave that place and retrace your steps. Go back to the Kynoch, back to your friends, back to those wonderful, erotic women. They will be worried. They will be waiting for you. If you listen you might hear them call your name. You do remember your name? If you listen closely you may hear their cries and feel their anguish.

You turn your face into the fog and you wait. *He will come, he must come, he gave you his word.*

You remember your big manor house. You remember your wife. You remember your children. They too will be waiting for you. They too will be worried if you do not return to them. In despair you punch the air and soundlessly cry out their names.

A lone fisherman, in readiness for the returning tide, patiently sits by the sea wall. Something shimmers in the darkness. He blinks and it is gone. He shrugs and returns to his thoughts.

You see no-one. You hear no-one. Your face remains fixed on the thickening miasma.

You consider. You hear your thoughts and you consider. The wind direction shifts slightly. The tide returns. Water now washes the shingle beneath you. A fog horn sounds once more. Its vibrations feel more intense. It must be him. It can only be him. The rain eases. You sense the approaching dawn. You have hope. At last you have hope. *He will come, he must keep his word.*

You heard his voice in your head. He called your name. He screamed your name. In blind panic, you ran. You opened the garden door and you ran. His words burnt into your brain. He promised that he would return to complete that which you started. You ran. In terror you ran. You ran out onto those cold, damp, rotting timbers and you leapt.

You sit on that same jetty, facing outwards towards the river's open mouth. The sun is setting, casting thin red lines over the receding tide. Gulls scavenge deep into the cold, wet mud for morsels of black nourishment. Every day you sit on those weathered planks. Every day you wait.

You need not concern yourself. He will keep his promise, but he has no need to rush. He knows where you are. Until he comes you will always be there waiting. Waiting for him to claim that which you sold to him.

You will not see him through those bird pecked holes. You will not hear him through those fish eaten stubs. But yes, be assured, he will return to wrench that wretched, corrupted soul from deep within your vile spirit. Only then will you truly learn the meaning of torment. Only then will all such feelings of hope, be twisted from within your screaming skull. Until that time comes you will remain on those cold, wet planks and fester within your own private hell.

With thanks to Geoff Barsby (District News Editor) whose article planted the seed that inspired me to write this piece.

Poem 4

Tracey Phillips

You're a big girl now,
Mummy said,
as she got me out of bed,
It's time to get dressed,
Come on run,
You can't be the last one.

But what if I don't like it,
What if they're mean
Do I have to keep my clothes nice and clean?

What will I do, if I wet myself,
Or can't reach the top of a shelf?
What if no one wants to play
And shouts at me to go away?

Hush now darling, you'll be ok,
They'll be your friends and want to play
It's going to be good, it'll be cool,
I know that you will love being at school!

100 Worder: Don't Call Me

Julie Kendall

I felt the chill. It was him again. I should put the phone down. I was at work after all.
Put it down.
I don't.
It stays firmly in my shaking hand. Every day he would call me. On leaving work I prayed he was not waiting for me. I felt I was being followed, step by step. "Gill, talk to me, please. I am sorry."
I ran from this pervert. He had touched me when I was ten, messed up my life forever, been in prison. Now he was out and my brother would never be a brother again.

Limerickish

Peter Sandling

Obsessed Charlotte Dunning
Was so keen on running
A blur of lycra and carbs
But her sudden double vision
Caused an ironic collision
With a lorry carrying Marathon bars.

Crass Arthur Spittle
Was the opposite of little
Who commanded respect from the few
He dominated his wife
Who retaliated in life
In bed with a man from the Pru.

Penny Dreadful: Little Red Riding Hood

Vicky Jacobson

The child had been distracted on her way to her grandmother's house.

She had arrived too late.

Neighbours heard the commotion from a mile away and when the police arrived, they found the front door standing wide open. The sharp, coppery smell of blood hung in the air and a few smears marked the walls at the top of the staircase.

The bedroom though was worse. Blood, splashed up the walls and across the ceiling, dripped down to form sticky puddles on the floor; red footprints were everywhere and the stench was overpowering.

An elderly woman had been found, half in and half out of bed, her throat ripped out and her once white nightgown shredded into tatters and saturated with blood. Wounds on her body showed that something with very long, very sharp teeth and claws had been enjoying itself immensely. One of the younger policemen retched and stumbled backwards out of the room, a hand clasped firmly over his mouth. He seemed oblivious to the fact that he'd almost knocked the senior officer over in his rush to leave.

On the floor, by the side of the bed, lay a man. Splattered and bloodied, he wore no clothes and looked as though he'd been hacked to death with something sharp.

A young PC with sandy hair and freckles bent down and picked up a small axe lying beside the body. "'Ere you go Sir, a likely culprit I'd say." He looked quite pleased with himself.

The sergeant looked at it disdainfully, "Yeah, I don't think so, Mullins – look," he pointed to the inscription on the blade, "and it doesn't even have a proper edge. I'd be very surprised if that caused the damage."

"But, Sarge, it's smeared with blood."

The sergeant sighed, "So is everything else, Mullins, so is everything else." He still reached for an evidence bag, though.

"Excuse me, Sir." A uniformed policeman put his head round the door. "Something you need to see."

On the landing, the door to the airing cupboard was standing open. Right at the back, in the tiny space beside the hot water tank, they'd found a small girl wearing a red hooded cloak. Her eyes were squeezed tightly shut and she clutched an old, battered teddy. There was a lot of blood on her clothes but, apart from a small wound to her arm, which the medic thought might be a bite, she didn't appear to have suffered any harm – well, nothing physical at least.

Later identified as the murdered woman's granddaughter, when they asked her what had happened, the child just covered her eyes and refused to answer. It was an extremely long time before she spoke again.

The dead man in the bedroom was confirmed to be one Norman Briggs, a man in his thirties who'd lived with his mother until she died a couple of years before.

When subsequently interviewed, all his neighbours professed surprise at Norman's involvement in such a heinous crime.

"Such a quiet, pleasant man," they'd said, and "of course, he kept himself to himself but we always thought he was so nice."

When it came down to it though, it seemed that nobody really knew the man who lived at number 26. The woman across the street volunteered the information that he generally kept his curtains drawn. Mrs Murphy, who lived on the corner, said she'd noticed he had a tendency to go out late at night sometimes, but everybody else just expressed total shock that Norman could be responsible for such an attack.

However they looked at it, the police could not work out what really happened that night but eventually they decided that Norman's nocturnal trips must be connected to all the burglaries in the area. The lack of evidence for this conclusion was conveniently overlooked because it meant the chief could clear some of his massive backlog of unsolved cases – he was seen rubbing his hands together and helping himself to a nice, fat cigar.

When one of the investigators raised the subject of Norman's lack of clothes, the best guess was that the man was obviously some sort of pervert whose thoughts had turned to rape when he'd broken into the house and found a woman alone in bed.

"We found his clothes ripped and torn on the kitchen floor," said the chief, "and that alone is clear evidence of the man's frenzied appetites."

One of the younger policemen – though not PC Mullins nor the green-faced lad who'd left in a hurry – had pointed out that the woman had to be in her late eighties at least.

The chief had waved that away with an airy, "I know it's shocking, son, but trust me, it happens."

So, without any real evidence to go on, the case was shelved and the child, dubbed Little Red Riding Hood by the press because of her red cloak, was placed in an institution. This was thought for the best as nobody was really sure what part she might have played in the carnage and she wasn't able to tell them. In due course, the world put the matter to the back of its collective mind.

The years went by; the little girl grew into a big girl and gradually recovered from the traumatic events which had led her to the institute. The approach of her eighteenth birthday led the clever men in charge of such things to decide – undoubtedly with a close eye to the savings such a move would make – that she was now fit to go back into the world. Probably best to give her a new identity, they said, after all, people tend to have long memories when it comes to grisly murders.

Besides, it wasn't as if there was anybody left to care by this time anyway. The child's only living relative had been her mother and she'd been a screw-up well before the tragedy occurred. They did make a token effort to find her but nobody'd heard from her in years and there were rumours that she'd overdosed in some alley a long time ago.

The girl herself had no recollection of her past, all she knew was that she'd been at the institute for a very long time. Once known by the colour of her cloak, she'd grown into a lovely young woman. Slender with flowing, light-brown hair, she had a dreamy, other-worldly quality with a grace and fluidity of movement which gave her an oddly sensual vibe. Despite her allure, she never had to endure the sort of harassment suffered by others from those whose interest in their charges was, shall we say, less than wholesome: one look from those calm, golden eyes was enough to curb the lust of any would-be predator. Strangely, had anybody cared enough to check, they would have seen her admittance form stated quite clearly that her eyes were blue.

As the girl got older, she sometimes found herself drawn to the window at night to look up at the moon. A strange longing would surge through her then and it got stronger and stronger the closer she got to her eighteenth birthday.

The first time she changed, the girl was terrified. Shortly after her birthday, she awoke suddenly to find the full moon shining through the window onto her bed. A suffocating pressure began to build within her and she found it hard to breathe. Sudden intense pain radiated through her limbs and the scar on her arm began to burn and glow.

Her first thought was that she was suffering a heart attack as scenes from her past flashed through her mind – visions tumbled one over another: she saw herself skipping through the woods, her basket full of goodies to take to her grandmother, looking forward to the cake and milk that Granny always gave her; she saw a tall man with a long face approach her and point out the pretty wild flowers she could pick as a gift; then she was in her grandmother's bedroom with the wolf and she saw how he'd cornered her and whispered what he was going to do to her with his big teeth. She saw how her small hands had found her grandfather's hand axe – the axe that had been inscribed and silver-plated by grateful employers on his death – and how, in desperation, she'd swung it at the wolf, hitting him again and again. At the time she'd had no idea that the silver coating had saved her life; now she understood intuitively how lucky that had been. She relived the pain she'd felt when the wolf had bitten her in their struggle and, for the first time, knowledge of what that meant dawned.

With that realisation came the awareness that she had to get out of the room before her transformation was complete. She quietly raised the window and slipped outside into the cool night air. Hurriedly stumbling across the grass to a secluded growth of dense thicket, she quickly pulled off her nightdress and hid it beneath the branches. Then she curled up and surrendered, for the first time, to the feelings running through her.

The girl awoke in the thicket the following morning. Her legs and feet were muddy and scratched and she could taste rabbit's blood in her mouth. She couldn't say how she knew it was from a rabbit but she knew it in the same way that she knew her wounds would heal rapidly.

She thought back to the exhilaration she'd felt, loping through the night, the damp forest air on her skin and the feelings of strength and empowerment. The blood of the Lycan, which she knew now coursed through her veins, had awakened the race memories of those ancient creatures. Unable to resist, she threw back her head and howled with joy. If anybody heard she was sure they'd assume it was just a dog.

There were many things which came instinctively with her newfound knowledge and many things she would need to learn. She knew she would have to seek out others like herself to teach her those skills to help keep their existence a secret from the rest of humanity.

The first task now, though, would be to get back to her room and clean herself before the world awoke.

Everything else could come in due course…

Karmic Seas

Bianca Eleanor

Longing to let go…
inhibitions.
Be brave and dive in.

I float,
wading through your waters,
Too far from shore.

Trust.

You lend me your wounds under moonlight,
Time escapes us,
Everything else is noise.

We build bridges over broken walls,
labour-less.
No armour.

You leave fingerprints on my naked soul,
And tattoos of destiny on my heart.

Distance.

The scent of dawn, and sunlight,
dance over you, as you rise from my bed.
Torment.

Betrayal.

You leave me with ink stains,
your name on poems, unwritten,
I can't erase.

Lost.
Celestial tides bring you home,
in full bloom.

Bound to you I return,
safe in your harbour,
sailing through stardust.

Complete.

Dedication: For Adam Isherwood; Rosie and Jim1.0.

High as a Kite

Paul Westgate

I put the books on the counter. Bobby was starting to hop from foot to foot, excited and impatient to get to the park.

"Ten dollars," I said, "and we get a free kite."

The woman nodded, opening each book in turn and adding up the prices pencilled on the flyleaves on a small calculator.

"Nine fifty," she said, "no kite."

Bobby stopped hopping and looked stricken.

"No, I'm sure it was ten," I said. "Could you check please?"

The woman sighed and went through the books again, this time subtracting the prices from the total still showing on the calculator's display. I saw it return to zero after the last price was taken off.

"Nine fifty," she repeated, "no kite."

"Look," I said, "he'll enjoy the books but right now he really wants to play with the kite. He's had his heart set on it. What do you say?"

The woman didn't say anything, just gave me a look. It was a look that said she'd heard it all before, didn't buy it then and wasn't buying it now.

"OK," I said, "how about I give you ten for the books anyway and you give me the kite?"

"No, can't do that," she said, "messes up my accounting."

She gave a thin smile "Most folks want a discount." The smile vanished. "I don't do that either. Messes up my accounting. You could choose another book, that would do it."

"Can we, Gramps?" Bobby asked. "Can we get another book?"

The shelves I'd looked through had books priced from two dollars to five. I expected Bobby would like a soda or something after the park and there was still the bus fares home. I looked down at Bobby, his eyes bright with hope.

138

"Don't sell those," I said, pointing to the books. "I'll be just a minute."

I started to walk back to the shelves. There was an open bin of books I hadn't noticed before. They appeared to have been thrown in carelessly, which was no way to treat books. I glanced down and there it was, right on top, *Conversations* by Robert A. Clark. Published nearly fifty years ago and out of print for almost as long, it still looked in pretty good condition. I picked it up and opened it. "To Anthony," I read, "with Best Wishes" and a scrawled signature. It was priced at fifty cents.

I didn't remember Anthony but I must have signed upwards of fifty books that day. That was an exciting time; receiving my author's copy, reading all the stories as if for the first time, the book signing, the royalty cheque that I'd never cashed. My copy was long gone, loaned and never returned, the original manuscript lost during the divorce upheaval. Bobby was too young for it but in a few years it would be OK for him. I'd add another dedication and give it to Alice to keep until he was older. I reckoned he'd like something from his old Gramps's past. The high point as well. I walked back to the counter and added the book to the pile.

"Ten dollars," I said, "and we get a free kite."

The woman checked the price. "Ten dollars," she confirmed, "you get the kite."

I put a five and five singles on the counter. She gathered them up, put them in a drawer and wrote today's date and a neat '$10.00' in a small notebook. She pushed the books across the counter to me, turned and reached for a cellophane covered package. She handed it to Bobby, a broad grin now on his face.

Bobby headed off towards the door, once again hopping from foot to foot. I followed, holding the books against my chest, *Conversations* on top. I felt the excitement of fifty years ago. It would be good to read the stories again. Halfway to the door, I hopped from one foot to the other.

139

About the Authors

Bianca Eleanor

Bianca has a BA (Hons) in Fashion Communication Marketing Promotion. She is also a fully qualified crystal therapist and Tantra student. She lives by the sea, with fellow writer, Adam Isherwood, and their two young sons, amongst many rocks and tiny robots.

She joined Canvey Writers earlier this year, with this being her first return to creative writing since winning a poetry competition at the age of seven.

Bianca loves hip-hop, vintage 2D fighters, Buffy the Vampire Slayer, and sacred geometry. She is a collector of Tarot/Oracle decks and X-Men comics.

In her spare time she likes to debate and study the historical character Anne Boleyn in online forums, or get lost in the world of Thra. She is most happy exploring museums after a visit to China Town or the Häagen-Dazs café in London.

Janice Gilbert

Janice will be the first to admit she is a frustrated writer who has yet to produce a story. She confesses to being a grammar geek, punctuation pedant and spelling specialist, suffering from apostrophobia and semi-colitis.

She recently gave up a "good" nine-to-five job to follow her heart and be a freelance copy-editor and has contributed to the polishing of many of the stories in this book. She advises: **Practice safe text: use commas.**

Debz Hobbs-Wyatt

Debz Hobbs-Wyatt is an award-winning short story writer, published novelist, professional editor and small publisher.

She has been published in twenty-five short story collections, was nominated for the prestigious US Pushcart Prize, shortlisted in the Commonwealth Short Story Prize and won the inaugural Bath Short Story award. She edits for short story publisher, Bridge House Publishing.

Her debut novel *While No One Was Watching* was published by Parthian Books in 2013 and her agent is currently seeking homes for her next novels. When not writing, she works as professional editor – privately and for Cornerstones Literary Consultancy. Debz founded and currently chairs Canvey Writers. She also loves Barry Manilow!

Phil Horscroft

Phil has been a Royal Marine, a milkman, a bus driver, an insurance salesman, an offshore wealth manager, a teacher in a prison (as a member of staff), and back to bus driver in that order. One day he hopes to decide what to be when he grows up. Father of two and doting grandfather of the three most wonderful people ever to be born, he lives in Essex and enjoys not owning a television, which allows him to torment the TV Licensing Agency, as well as keeping unfit and eating cakes.

Adam Isherwod

Adam Isherwood, self-published author of the *Shattered Verse* Sci-Fi tabletop game, is a recent addition to the Canvey Writers group. His debut short story *Legion of One* is part of a larger project which he hopes to evolve into an epic saga. Also a keen historian and wargame enthusiast who runs the local tabletop gaming club, Iron Forest Games.

Alan Jacobson

Alan is a retired IT Project Manager. His interests include music, technology and photography. He invented the fork and blotting paper and is currently building a time travel machine. Alan is unpublished, unappreciated, unloved and prone to exaggeration and lying.

Vicky Jacobson

Vicky is a retired legal secretary with two grown up children, one of whom still lives at home. She has always wanted to write and, spotting an ad for a new writing group, she took a deep breath and joined Canvey Writers, hoping for inspiration. Luckily the move seems to have proved successful as she has since had two of her short stories published online at Café Lit, and was absolutely delighted when both were picked for that year's anthology.

She is married to Alan Jacobson and confirms everything he said in his bio but says he omitted to add that he is an avid collector of tools, which look very nice on the shelves of his shed. She hopes that one day he might actually put some of them to use and build something.

Vicky is very pleased to announce that she recently passed her driving test, after many, many hours of lessons and a lifetime of procrastination. She disputes the suggestion that this should be taken as a warning.

Julie Kendall

Julie enjoys writing poems and short stories as a pleasurable pastime. She has such a vivid imagination, she says her mind can't get it onto the paper quickly enough and she can knock up a short story in half an hour! She likes writing, whether true to life stories or romantic ones. Also she likes writing limericks. She says it always reminds her of her dad who used to write them years ago.

In her free time, Julie enjoys nothing more than walking along the seafront at Canvey where she lives, and being in the garden or walking through a field and seeing wild flowers. Nature is something so beautiful; we take it for granted but we need to make the time to stop and stare.

Henry Lewi

Henry is a semi-retired Urological Surgeon, having qualified from the Welsh National School of Medicine many years ago. He did his surgical training in Cardiff, Edinburgh and Glasgow and has worked in the NHS for over thirty years. Having recently completed an MA in Military History at the University of Birmingham, he is now continuing his studies at the University of Wolverhampton. Whilst he has written and published many scientific articles over the years, this is his first attempt at writing fiction.

Robert Parker

On retiring from the Metropolitan Police Service in 2009, Bob became interested in writing. Keen to save the world from yet another set of policeman's memoirs, he turned to his other interest – South Africa. Helped by his wife, Linda, the first Georgina van Wyk mystery, *The SA Connection* was published in October 2015, followed by *A Case of South African Reds* in September 2017. He is currently working on *Georgie and the Voortrekkers* to complete the trilogy. All three books are well researched political thrillers set in 1960s South Africa.

Tracey Phillips

Tracey is an adopted Essex-girl. She's a qualified nursery nurse who loves writing random rhymes. She's also a passionate supporter of breast cancer research and her lifelong plans are to one day write and publish her varied collection of rhymes and to marry Robbie Williams.

Margaret Potter

Margaret Potter has enjoyed writing for a number of years. She has had several short stories published in *Woman's Weekly* Fiction magazine and seen her work in their Yearbook.

She was shortlisted in the Saga Ghost competition 2014 and her children's story *Pirate Bill* won the "Be a Write Pirate" competition run by the Penzance Literary Festival 2014.

She has been published in several children's publications and one of her stories for children has been printed in braille for the RNIB.

Her story *The Perfectionist*, included in this anthology, was inspired by a writing prompt given at one of the Canvey Writers' enjoyable meetings for like-minded people.

Peter Sandling

Peter has been writing short stories and poetry for a number of years. He likes to include subject matter from all areas of life and is particularly interested in people's reactions to specific situations and tries to incorporate these in his work. He has a varied interest in literature and is a member of a crime reading group. He runs a small, informal writing group fortnightly at Canvey Library on Tuesday afternoons, and tries to encourage members in their creative projects.

He was very pleased to have a short story published in CaféLit. Peter is married with two adult sons. He says that all family members are artistically and musically talented but his only contribution during musical get-togethers is his proficiency on the washboard and paper and comb.

Peter is a keen bowls player and enjoys every moment of his retirement.

Amber Graelin

Amber has been writing short stories and poetry since she was very young and had her first poem published professionally aged fifteen. She is primarily a poet and often writes "in the moment" in order to capture and exploit the raw emotions she has felt at a particular instant or because of a specific situation. Amber writes predominantly for herself due to the personal nature of the subject matters she chooses, however, she has found that sharing within the writing group has been an excellent outlet at times. She has kept diaries for most of her life in the hopes that one day she will write her life story and tell it to the world.

Gini Scanlan

Gini Scanlan is a full-time Project Engineer with a part-time passion for writing which sustains her lifelong love affair with words. After completing two creative writing modules with The Open University, Gini has begrudgingly come to the conclusion that she is never going to write a novel. However, she enjoys writing poetry and short pieces of fiction, so all is not lost. Her free time is spent crafting or composing short stories and poems, as well as taking care of her ever-growing family; one husband, four children, two grandchildren and a small menagerie.

Dave Traer

Dave began life in Bethnal Green. He later married and ventured east towards the sea. His London upbringing and many years as a site electrician have given him a sometimes off-the-wall view of characters, who continue to enhance his storylines. With an ability to present the unexpected, he finds enjoyment in his writing, an emotion which intensifies when others appreciate his work.

Further examples of Dave's work can be found at the daytime Canvey Writers Group website. The next hundred words have been reserved for his future publishing triumphs!

Paul Westgate

Paul was born and brought up in Essex and spent his working life in London. He is married and continues to live in Essex. He began fiction writing after attending a writing course in 2011 and regularly contributes to creativecafe.blogspot.co.uk and other online magazines. He was delighted to have a short story published in *The Best of CaféLit 5* in 2016. As well as writing, Paul pursues an eclectic mix of activities and is cultivating a 1920s gentleman's lifestyle.

Colin Wyatt

Colin has spent his working life as a children's illustrator, which has included designing the visual concept for *The Poddington Peas* which became an animated series shown regularly on BBC Television. He also illustrated such well-known characters as "Noddy" and "Thomas the Tank Engine". He has worked for Walt Disney Productions for more than twenty years, producing artwork for Disney publications such as annuals and weekly comics.

Colin's writing career began in 2011 when he wrote and illustrated *The Jet-Set*, a picture book series published by Paws n Claws Publishing, about four super-hero animal characters that help wild animals in trouble.

Colin's latest book, which, again, he has both written and illustrated, is *Who will be my FRIEND?* published by Chapeltown Books.

Index of Authors

Afterword and Acknowledgements

We really hope you've enjoyed this varied collection of the work of Canvey Writers St Nicholas Group and we thank you for purchasing this book. By doing so, you are supporting a talented bunch as well helping our chosen charity.

If you live in Essex and close to Canvey Island then please feel free to get in touch and find out more about our group. You can email me (Debz) writer@debzhobbs-wyatt.co.uk

Or why not look online as there is sure to be a writing group near you.

I really want to thank everyone in the group and connected to the group for their support with this project... especially Gini and Janice who have been invaluable in putting this collection together and editing it for you!

Other Publications by Bridge House

Snowflakes

edited by Debz Hobbs-Wyatt and Gill James

Our theme for 2015 is snowflakes. Stories that contain snowflakes and that are like snowflakes. Unique and perfectly formed. As they melt into the psyche they bring a life-sustaining force. Snow can be beautiful and it can be treacherous. It can swing from one extreme to another in seconds. It is an important part of the nature cycle. Here you will find that our writers have risen to the challenge.

"Great collection of fresh, innovative and moving stories. Best read near a roaring fire, as some of the stories are chilling indeed. Highly recommended" (*Amazon*)

Order from www.bridgehousepublishing.co.uk

Paperback: ISBN 978-1-907335-40-2
eBook: ISBN 978-1-907335-41-9

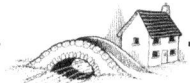

Baubles

edited by Debz Hobbs-Wyatt and Gill James

The challenge was to write a bauble of a story. So we have a
varied selection of snippets that sparkle. Once again we feel
privileged to publish this fine group of writers. Each story is
different and glitters in its own way.

"A great range of stories and styles here. A story for everyone.
Talented, contemporary writers writing about issues that
engage you." (*Amazon*)

Order from www.bridgehousepublishing.co.uk

Paperback: ISBN 978-1-907335-46-4
eBook: ISBN 978-1-907335-47-1